No Edges

No Edges

Swahili Stories

CALICO

No Edges is seventh in the Calico Series.

Two Lines Press
582 Market Street, Suite 700, San Francisco, CA 94104
www.twolinespress.com

ISBN: 978-1-949641-45-5

Cover design by Crisis
Cover image © Thandiwe Muriu
Typesetting and interior design by LOKI
Printed in the United States of America

THIS BOOK WAS PUBLISHED WITH SUPPORT
FROM THE NATIONAL ENDOWMENT FOR THE ARTS.

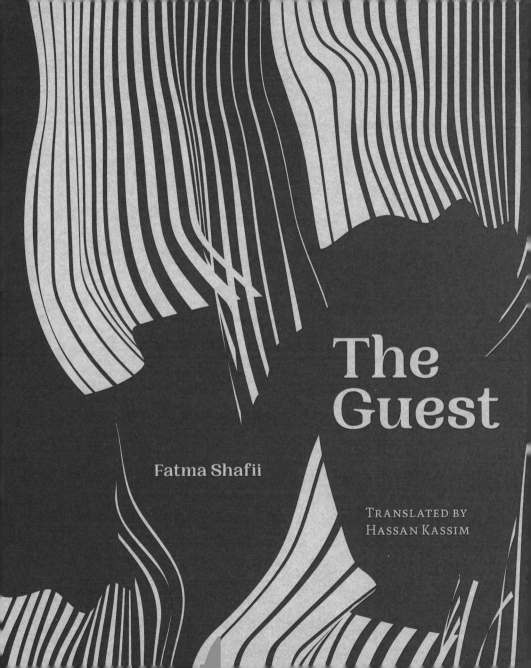

The
Guest

Fatma Shafii

TRANSLATED BY
HASSAN KASSIM

Kichwa kilimzunguka
kama tiara. Hofu ilimvaa.
Alishika kitutu. *Kwanini
hajawasili?* Aliwaza.

IT WAS LATE AT NIGHT AND THE DARKNESS WAS FAR-reaching. The wind was relentless; the rain gushed; the thunder pounded haphazardly. There was the frequent clatter of utensils falling, as unlatched windows closed and opened violently in the wind. Tick tock tick tock, time marched. The girl emerged exhausted from the world of sleep. Getting to her feet, she walked to the window, parted the curtains, and peeked outside. Then returned to bed, pulling up the sheets halfway. She glanced at the clock by the far corner of her bed: a quarter to two. She widened her eyes in disbelief and looked back outside. Silence. Her head was spinning like a kite. Her nerves were racked. *Why hasn't he arrived yet?* she wondered, fingering her neck.

It was highly unusual for him to be this late. She thought maybe it was because of the rain.

She could no longer sit still. Notwithstanding the cold wind coming from the open window, a thin trickle of sweat was running from her armpit. She did not understand what was happening. Making her way to her brother's room, she found him fast asleep. She shook him at least three times, but he did not wake, so she left him and headed toward her parents' room. From the doorway, she could hear them snoring. Everyone was asleep. She returned to her room.

After much cajoling and convincing, at last he had agreed to meet her parents. They planned to make the introduction that coming dawn. A desire had ignited within her, to prove to everyone that she was a woman of honor, that she had in fact been telling the truth about her beloved. She'd *show* her brother, who teased her daily that she was turning into an old maid who still lived in her parents' house; and her mother, who persistently tried to marry her off to men of different descents: Swahili, Arab, and once, an Indian. Each time, she refused. She utterly refused, insisting there was already a young man ready to marry her and she'd introduce him to them very soon.

Two-thirty in the morning and still he hadn't showed. She decided to distract herself with frivolous acts, preparing herself to receive her beloved, her soon-to-be husband. In the bathroom, she bathed in tepid water and dressed herself in her most elegant clothes. She put on the silver earrings her beloved liked—the ones he complimented whenever she wore them—then spritzed herself with the most enticing perfume. Last, she pulled a chair out from behind the door and placed it opposite her bed. For her guest.

Their relationship had been going on for a while now. She remembered the first time they'd met. At nine at night, she'd rushed out to purchase sanitary pads from the shop. Her flow had suddenly started gushing and they'd had no spare pads at home. It was as she was leaving the store that, though she was in a hurry to get back, the man wore her down and got to talk to her for a few minutes. And that was how, casually, they'd gotten to know each other and grown closer. She'd been scared at first. She wouldn't utter a single word around him. But recently, a familiarity had settled between them. They'd sit together conversing, laughing, him drawing her into the comfort of an embrace. And his behavior of late had only caused her love for him to grow. She now had her hair stroked, a new experience for her, her hands held, her palms kissed. On those evenings when he arrived late, their exchanges were scant, and she'd fall asleep to him caressing her back. His tardiness did not concern her, for he'd already explained he worked the evening shift late into the night. These encounters ushered in sensations wholly new to her. Feelings that crawled into her veins and made her entire body tingle with excitement. She delighted in them. Saw the night as day and day as night. She'd be distracted all day long, engrossed in thoughts of the previous night or else daydreaming about what he would do to her that coming evening.

Her girlfriends were most eager to meet this suitor, for she sang of him with a devotion usually reserved for the national anthem, all without confirmation of his existence. Day after day, she'd tell them how refined her man was, his head shaved stylishly and his beard properly trimmed. Some believed her, but others dismissed her as a liar, and still others said she had lost it. What baffled them most was that supposedly the man wasn't even from their village, but rather passed through each night after work headed for his place in the neighboring village. They were flummoxed: How could she be acquainted with a boy from somewhere else when she herself had never left! What's more, she often grew conceited; there was no way her beloved was duplicitous like so many of the men in their village. Time alone would help her friends solve the riddle.

That which is long anticipated eventually comes to pass. At three o'clock on the dot, the guest she'd been awaiting with bated breath finally arrived. She received him with unbridled exuberance, frantic, jubilant, genial, her hands fluttering. Her heart, previously hammering with apprehension, now pulsated with delight. She'd known he wouldn't miss his appointment.

She believed so much in this man, knew that the love she had for him would never permit him to break his promise.

Like always, the man sat in the chair facing her in bed. Then he took her hands in his and covered her palms with kisses. She melted, as all her worries from earlier vaporized. And then she smiled.

"Oh, my darling, my most honored one," the guest began. "How are you?"

"*Alhamdulillah*," she answered.

"Please forgive my lateness today. There was a bit of a situation, and I was forced to attend to it."

"What was it, love?"

"The man with the shift after me had a family emergency. I had no choice but to cover for him until he arrived."

"It does not matter, so long as you're here. Are you aware that today is our big day?"

"I'm well aware, but..."

She cut him off. "No my love, please no excuses today. I already promised Mother. At dawn, I will introduce you to her."

He stood and strode to the window, gazing outside, while she continued, "Today is today, and he who speaks of tomorrow lies. I cannot believe this day is finally here. I've been patient for so long. Truly, there is no ordeal so long that it won't come to an end. They will finally quit mocking me, saying I am unworthy of love. At school, they say I'm not pretty. Just two days ago, I passed a group of boys at a *maskani* and heard them call me mad. I can't wait to see the look on my brother's face when you address Mother, to witness his shock. I can't believe they don't believe me. Where did I go wrong?"

Now on her feet, she felt him approach from behind and press against her. Her eyes were tearing up and her lips curled into a smile. Turning around, she lay her palm on her lover's cheek, stared into his eyes, and said, "I feel the time has come for me to wed. I think you'll find I'm emotionally mature and able to take good care of you. I do not want to grow old in this house while my friends are off getting married and having children. All I want is for you to marry me. That is my deepest desire. You bring me so much comfort and don't tease me like all the others."

The man moved closer and planted a kiss on her forehead. They became entangled in an embrace, fell into bed, and pulled up the covers.

"If I may," she said, "where would you like to get married?"

"Wherever," he said. "I'm only opposed to a long ceremony, for I long too fondly. I want to marry you and take you away with me. You'll come live with me, and I promise you will not regret it. I'll make you happy beyond compare."

"Where is that?"

"Where I'm from. Where there is no annoyance, no cause for

distress, no end to things—we'll live forever, just you and me."

"Enough of your sarcasm, can anything really be so? Everything has its end. What I want is to live with you for my remaining days."

Together, they laughed.

"You know, I've been lost in thought day in and day out, imagining our wedding with every free moment I get. I know Mother will organize a grand ceremony, since I am her only daughter, and besides, she has her reputation to maintain. Our wedding will be so flooded with visiting dignitaries that the village will tremble," she finished.

"You're getting ahead of yourself," he laughed.

They kept chatting and romancing, while time passed.

Whether the rooster crows or not, the sun will rise! Daybreak ripened and the hour of morning knocked, the holy sun splintering its rays onto the farthest horizon and bidding the dawn farewell. The girl's mother left her room and began her day's work as she did every morning. She prepared her husband's bathwater and placed his towel in the bathroom, then walked to her son's room and roused him, informing him that he was already late for the morning prayer. The bustle of the day began. One after another the members of the household awoke, save for the girl.

"Is that girl still asleep? Isn't the sun beating down on her in that room?" the mother asked in a raised voice as if addressing the whole neighborhood. She marched straight to her daughter's room and opened the door.

"Surpriiiiiiiiiisssseeeee," the daughter sang, smiling.

She gestured toward her beloved's hand.

"Mother, as promised, meet the love of my life. We've been waiting most eagerly for you to wake."

"My God!" the mother cried.

"I knew you'd be startled. Even I'm trembling. This matter of introducing your beloved to your parents is not as easy as I'd anticipated."

She walked to stand next to her man.

"My love, this is my mother, *kipenzi changu*, your soon-to-be mother-in-law. Go on, don't be afraid, she's alright."

"My child! Isn't that just the bed?"

"Aah Ma, please don't tease me. I'm serious right now."

"Why am I not seeing anyone?"

"Ma, you must still be half asleep."

"*Ya Ilahi!*" exclaimed the mother. "This cannot be! Swaleheeee, oh Swaleheee!"

"*Naam,*" responded the young man from across the hall.

"Go and get your father. I see the water has exceeded the flour in this girl."

"Is she at it again?" Swaleh asked.

"And gone beyond. Hurry, call him in here."

The girl dropped to the ground and began wailing.

"My love, speak up. Don't you see? Didn't I tell you they wouldn't believe me? I'm tired. Tired of this life."

She thrust her head to the floor and wept ardently, tears streaming and mucus dripping.

A Neighbor's Pot

Lusajo Mwaikenda Israel

TRANSLATED BY
RICHARD PRINS

Usiku milio ya ngoma *ndu ndu ndu, kinkidi nkidi kinkindi nkidi* husikika kwa mbali toka mbuyuni hapo.

It's daybreak in the village of Kipwete, five o'clock at the crack of dawn, a gentle sun beginning to rise. Mama Chausiku, wife of the late Chaurembo, a widow with only one child, is in her kitchen pouring tea into a tin cup, the kind they give you in the clink. The wood stove is blowing smoke in her face, the way a wobbly ceiling fan blows dust around the room at a no-tell motel. Her eyes are red, like she just blazed uncured bud. With a soft voice, she calls her daughter Chausiku, *Chauu, my only child, come get your tea, it's time for school. Education is the key to life, girl. These days, if you don't hit the books, everyone thinks you're a dumb buoy.* Chausiku, squinting with sleep, responds in a drowsy voice, *Yeah, Mama, I'm coming, thank you, Mama.*

Chausiku is a medicine child; her mother went to a healer for an herbal remedy to help her conceive. Now she's fourteen years old and in her third year at Kikondo Secondary. This girl's a little bit mischievous, but she's serious about her studies.

She has a bestie, her neighbor Sikuzani, and the two of them are hitting the books hard to get through their third year at Kikondo. It's two kilometers and change from Chausiku's to school, which is all the way in the neighboring village of Nachele, so it takes a while to get there. Every day Chausiku and Sikuzani follow each other back and forth to and from school. They march single file, like termites, or lice. It's hard to tell them apart; the two of them look just like a pair of shoes.

Every morning before they roll into school, Chausiku and Sikuzani make the long trek through tangles of wilderness. Mama Chausiku and Mama Sikuzani don't want them fooling along the way. But their childish minds don't get it. They think it's all good to screw around; their mischief is in full bloom. Youth is nothing but boiling water, and a deaf ear can't hear its own cure.

On the way to school from Chausiku's house, there is a large baobab tree, a taboo baobab, where sorcerers gather regularly to cast their spells. At night the bellowing of drums can be heard from afar, *ndu ndu ndu, kinkidi nkidi kinkindi nkidi*, emanating from the direction of the baobab. This baobab has been around for ages and ages. Crews from different villages perform traditional rituals there, while all the wizards and whatnot use the tree as their forum. Debating and plotting their shady deeds.

One day that won't be named, Chausiku and Sikuzani are passing by the baobab. Some kids are there, shooting pebbles and playing ring-around-the-palm-fronds. So they toss their bags aside and join the fun. Of course, they don't realize that these aren't really children but wood sprites, planted there to entrap Chausiku. Suddenly, it starts sprinkling, followed by the rumble of thunder, *papapapa vuuuu, pu pu pu pu.* The other kids magically disappear, and Chausiku and Sikuzani break into a run. As they're booking it through the forest, Chausiku slips and falls on a shard from a cracked earthenware pot. And just like that, she's gone. Sikuzani loses it, howling, no idea what to do. She runs home, drenched by the rain, mud all down her legs.

When Sikuzani gets there, she's soaked and sobbing, hiccupping, gasping for breath, *Mama Mama Mama!* Mama Sikuzani and Mama Chausiku are chilling in the yard, chatting away. Spotting Sikuzani, a stunned Mama Chausiku asks her, *What's up with you, and where's your bestie?* Sikuzani, choking on tears, tries to speak, but no sound comes out. Her mother grabs her by the arm and drags her inside the house, followed by her friend, Mama Chausiku.

Inside, Sikuzani doesn't get out of her wet clothes or even wash her hands. She just sits down on the woven mat, her eyes rolling back like she's in a trance. Mama Chausiku pleads, *Speak up, what's going on?* And Sikuzani spills the whole story, beginning to end, of how Chausiku just up and disappeared. Mama Chausiku can't keep it together; her cheeks are drooping like a rat's fetus, tears flowing out of her like it's the rainy season. But Mama Sikuzani jumps in, all self-righteous, *I'm sorry, girlfriend, but you gotta get a grip, now!*

Mama Chausiku and Mama Sikuzani both go to see Mr. Chilu, the leader of their ten-house cell, and tell him what's happening. Mama Sikuzani's husband, Mr. Chogelo, has just come back from his field, scaring off the birds so they wouldn't eat up the rice paddy. Together, they all scour the village, searching for Chausiku. The authorities issue a public proclamation, and the whole village plunges into the forest to look for her, but it's no good.

*

On the day Chausiku disappeared into that hole, open and shut, she emerged in another town, like she was trapped in a dream and there was nothing she could do. This was the town of Galole, home to berserk and madcap witches. This town was full of trees, tall and short, and bushes of mesmerizing colors. There were cavernous walls festooned with human skulls and beastly crania. Among the strange growls and bird cries echoing around her, Chausiku could make out the distant sound of humans wailing.

Shaken and overwhelmed, she was at a loss of what to do. Just then, a two-headed giant with protuberant horns approached her, laughing, with a voice that quavered and echoed, *Welcome, little lady, you have arrived, little girl, hahaha!* Chausiku fainted. When she came to, she found herself inside a grass hut. Huddled in the corner were children just like her, except they had protracted fingernails and unnaturally long hair. Chausiku shivered, confused and frightened.

The next morning, a crone appeared, her face veiled in shadow. She wore a poor woman's shawl, black as night, plus a white turban, and she was gripping a red cloth. She grabbed Chausiku tightly by the arm, as the girl gulped *mnh mmmmnh.* She brought her to a field and sat her down on a stool. Two mountainous goons came and tied up her arms and legs. Chausiku had lost her cool and all her strength. Her body trembled, as she shed tears of fright.

The hag tattooed Chausiku all over her body using a razor dipped in the wizards' proprietary elixir. Chausiku gargled in pain, *Uwiii mnhnh uwii, Mama I'm dying!* After that, she was force-fed a mixture of flour and witchy brew. She tried to refuse, but they gripped her by the gullet and made her drink, the way you force someone who ingested poison to chug milk so they won't croak. After gulping down the flour mixture, Chausiku passed out, overcome by fear.

The next day Chausiku found herself back with the others in the grass hut. There they were visited by the lead sorcerer, who'd come to assign them their tasks. Chausiku and two of her fellows scored the job of mixing chaff, which they loaded onto carts pulled by hyenas. They mixed the chaff with blood and distributed it to all the other ensorcelled hostages in the village. They used human skulls as bowls, and desiccated hands as ladles to dish out all the bits and pieces.

In this village of sorcerers, hyenas were the main mode of transportation, and their bodies stank like rotting, sun-dried fish. There was also a large, blood-red lake where a bask of crocodiles fed on human flesh and animal carcasses. They were humongous, their teeth like jagged saws. If it ever happened that one of the hostages messed up, the sorcerers would grab them and fling them into the lake to be devoured by the possessed crocodiles. Certainly, it was a terrifying place.

The witches threw crazy parties where they binged on human flesh, and every six months, the village hosted the big wizard bash with the chief sorcerer as their honored guest. On that day, one hostage's throat would be slit, their blood passed among the sorcerers to drink, and a second hostage would be forced to imbibe as well. After that, they'd fry the first hostage, dunking their body in a large vat of boiling hot oil, providing the celebratory meal. The other hostage might be bound with rope and dunked in the vat, too, for seasoning.

The roar of the enchanted drums could now be heard, as all the sorcerers danced ecstatically, chanting, *Cha nchakara chakara cha nchakara chakara! Meat is sweet, blood is sweet! Meat is sweet, blood is sweet!* It was now four months since Chausiku had been taken, and that old hag, the one who'd tattooed her, had returned once more to the town of madcap witches. She whispered to Chausiku in a crepitating voice, *Today it's your turn.* Chausiku started choking with sobs, her spirit evaporating, as two wizards in red garments came and bound her hands and legs, dragging her off to the field where the party was to take place.

Once in the field, a woman stood before them, coated in soot and draped in a crimson blanket. She cackled and slashed each of Chausiku's cheeks with a razor. It was then that Chausiku peeped the woman's face. It was their neighbor, Mama Sikuzani. Chausiku's eyes popped out. She cried, *Mama, Mama, what did I do to you? Why would you hurt me?* Mama Sikuzani grabbed hold of Chausiku and began wrestling her toward the vat of oil in order to season their meal. Chausiku screamed, *Mamaaaa I'll die uwiiii!* The wizards pounded their enchanted drums and danced happily, while all the other hostages stood in a line, watching.

*

Four long months have gone by since Chausiku disappeared from the village. Mama Chausiku's sleep is shifty and unsettled. Chausiku often appears in her dreams and speaks to her, *Mama, Mama, help me, take me home! Mama, they're torturing me!* Then Mama Chausiku startles awake, drenched in sweat and shaking. This happens so often she can't enjoy anything. She just keeps losing weight and withering, lost in her own troubled mind. Remember, Chausiku was her only child, conceived with the aid of medicinal herbs.

Mama Chausiku ventures to a distant village named Gatore, where she calls on the ancestral faith healer known as Old Nandonde. Draped in red garments, a cap of ostrich feathers on his head, Old Nandonde welcomes her with a robust chuckle, *Hahaha my grandchild, welcome, Granddaughter.* Mama Chausiku replies, *Thank you, Grandfather,* as she enters his hut of palm fronds. The healer gestures for her to take a seat on the porcupine hide spread out on the floor.

Once seated, Mama Chausiku starts to tell the story of what has brought her there. Nandonde stops her. *Hahahaha, I know what brought you, I know everything! I know it's your daughter, haha! I know she can be found, I know she is alive, haha, I know!* Mama Chausiku sits there awestruck, her mouth wide open like it's the gate of the town marketplace.

The next morning a bright sun is gleaming in Mama Chausiku's village. The healer waddles alongside her all the way to the home of Mr. Chilu, the ten-house-leader. The healer asks for a black ewe, obedient, virginal, one that's never given birth. Mr. Chilu volunteers one of his own sheep. They lead the ewe to the baobab tree where Chausiku went missing and slit her throat, letting the blood soak the ground. The meat is served on a platter and all the villagers come and gorge themselves, piece by piece. Everyone is there except for Mama Sikuzani, her husband, and her daughter.

The healer announces that Chausiku will appear on the seventh day. And he reveals the truth of the matter: there is beef between Mama Chausiku and Mama Sikuzani. One day, long ago, Mama Chausiku hit up Mama Sikuzani for an earthenware pot, so she could boil her sweet potatoes. While Mama Chausiku was sifting rice, the pot fell to the ground—*puu paaa!*—and shattered into pieces. Mama Chausiku asked Mama Sikuzani to forgive her, it was just bad luck, she would buy her a new pot. But Mama Sikuzani refused, saying self-righteously, *Just drop it, neighbor, what's a pot, I have another.* But deep in her heart, she nursed a grudge, and nourished it with her hypocritical laughter. It's just like the Swahili say: human in sight, but not at heart. Or: the thing that's eating you is inside your own clothes. And so, Mama Sikuzani plotted her revenge, and being a sorcerer, she decided to exact it via her craft. So she set that enchanted shard of the cracked pot as a trap, there beside the baobab tree, and it was this that caused Chausiku's disappearance.

It's been seven days since the healer Old Nandonde administered his remedy. Back in the sorcerers' realm, Chausiku is about to be dumped in the vat of boiling oil when, suddenly, she faints. She wakes up in the corner of her kitchen. Mama Chausiku is walking in to grab a winnowing basket when she bumps smack into a strange creature, human but not human, zimwi but not zimwi; she lets out a startled scream.

Neighbors rush over. They come and marvel that it really is Chausiku. But Chausiku has changed; she has very long fingernails, each one like an old man's cane, plus hair resembling long stalks of dry corn. She can hardly speak in her feeble state. The neighbors take Chausiku and clean her up. They cut her nails and hair. They bathe her and dress her in new clothes, dazzling enough to make the whole village weep. They make her drink some of the potion Old Nandonde left for her. Her consciousness returns, and she embraces her mother, crying out in anguish, *Mama Mama Mama!* The village is astounded. They throw a party. They make celebratory offerings. They pound their drums. They eat and they drink. It's a giant, undying feast.

By then, Mama Sikuzani and her family are already on the road, fleeing to who knows where, since Mama Sikuzani surmised that her involvement in Chausiku's disappearance would be discovered. She is captured en route and brought back to the village. A meeting is convened. The healer Old Nandonde is summoned. Mama Sikuzani is shaved bald and forced to drink medicine to expel her magic. Same with her family. Her eyes bulge like a lizard stuck in a door. She weeps in disgrace, begging to be forgiven. People whisper in low voices, *Kick her out of the village! I mean, killing your friend's child over a pot? Like, it's just a pot! What kind of neighbor does that?* In the meeting it is decided that Mama Sikuzani and her family will be booted from the village. They walk away, hanging their heads in shame. Who knows where they go. That is the end of them.

Now time has passed and Chausiku is a straight-up babe, a real dish. She went back to school and finished her studies. Today she's a secretary at the post office, married, with two children. She is chilling in her living room when she hears a knock. She answers, *Come on in, but who is it?*

The one knocking replies, as if disguising their voice. *Neighbor! I've come to borrow a pot.*

Chausiku is alarmed. Opening the door, she finds herself face-to-face with—almost bumping into—her mother, who is paying an unexpected visit. They both burst out laughing. *You crack me up! A neighbor's pot!*

Mwas Mahugu

Translated from Sheng
by Idza Luhumyo

Timo and Kayole's Chaos

Morning K-town ilikua radiant, clear
sky na patches za clouds hapa na pale,
watoi busy wakienda chuo, mama
mbogas wakirudi kutoka soko, raia ya
industrial area, jeshi mathree taking
over the street, pia wasee wa kurauka
kwa vichinjio, Daggoreti.

Kayole Town is subdued, especially if you are coming from the other side of the city. And if you want to rejuvenate your mind, to reach that inner calm that you enjoy in nature, then it could be the perfect escape, only sometimes there is rapid gunfire exchanged between police officers and criminals. These kinds of street exchanges are fun for primary-school-age kids; ever since the schools closed for the winter holidays, they've been playing an alternative version of godi sinya, where they make guns with wire and rubber bands, and, in this way, entire days are spent playing cat-and-mouse in the K-Town alleys, with some of the naughty boys aiming at the buttocks of women. And they don't lack for games, for there is always taya, bano, and kati.

It's the street kids who really know something about hustle. They spend all day collecting cardboard, plastic bottles, and scrap metal. Sometimes, the estate kids stop their wire-gun games and scream in unison: "chokora mapipa chokora mapipa," and immediately, the petty wars begin, with each side shooting at the other. But the street kids always give up first because they are super-duper high from the glue bottles they carry around in their mouths, hanging from their lower lips. Somehow, the bottles never fall, no matter how fast the kids run.

The streets leading into K-Town are amazing, what with the artificial flowers in assorted colors, provided by the official department of garbage collection and arranged all over town in abstract designs. These officials also advised the citizens to pour soil on the road to cover the asphalt, but when it gets hot, the asphalt still burns the children's legs as they ride their bikes. This angers parents because their kids always return home with the same request: "Aaaaah woishe, Mama, could I please wear my school shoes just for today? I've gotten so many burns."

"NGRRRRi krriiiiiiiiiiiiiiiiiiiiiiiiiiiiiiiiiiiiing," goes the bell.

Ignoring the bell, they continue to play with their paper ball. It is afterschool free time, about four in the afternoon, and the middle schoolers have already gone home. The boys are having fun, but just then the teacher emerges out of nowhere!

"Hey boys, it's time to go home. Playtime is over, go home," the teacher announces loudly.

Timo quickly grabs the ball and, without responding, leaves, followed by the other boys. The teacher heads back to the classroom. Kayole Town Primary School is well-built, with concrete walls and gray asbestos roofing. It is a wonderful school.

After a couple of minutes, they reach the neighborhood and Timo slows down. They are breathing hard under the weight of their school bags on their backs.

Timo: Man, that teacher really spoiled our fun.

Friend: Timo man, I got you in a chobo! Haha!

Timo: Who? Who? Face like a chobo! Haha!

Friend: Have you started a roasting session?

Friend 2: It's on! I'm the referee.

They all form a circle and the roasting begins.

The sky is radiant. The sun's rays are casting a lovely golden-rust color over the neighborhood, as the sunset takes over. The mandazi vendors are about to start on their second round of the day. Rising early that morning, they served pastries to the fishmongers, mutura vendors, soup vendors, and nyama choma vendors, all the while hoping for more booming business later in the day; now people are coming home from work and the children are returning from school. The ice-cream vendor has been busy all day. The sun indicates to him that the time to close shop has come, that he is in the stoppage time. It is five in the evening.

As the sugarcane vendor passes, Baba Timo calls out to him.

"Cut a piece for us, one worth twenty shillings, and separate it into two portions," Baba Timo instructs the sugarcane vendor, before turning to his friend.

Baba Timo (clearing his throat): Oh Buddy, things have become so difficult.

Neighbor: It's not just difficult for you, it's that way for everyone, this is how life goes.

Baba Timo: I just can't believe my child turned out this way.

Neighbor: What has he done now?

Baba Timo: Nothing! He works hard in school, he's well-mannered. Buddy, I just pray to God that he gets into university!

The sugarcane vendor finishes cutting the sugarcane and is handing it to Baba Timo and his friend when, to both their surprise, they hear Timo say, "I want sugarcane too, Baba," and turn to see him crossing the yard toward them, carrying his school bag, a paper bag in his hand.

Baba Timo: Okay, cut up one worth ten shillings for him. (Turning to face his son.) Where are you coming from? Don't tell me you've been picking up that scrap metal too? Aaaha?

Timo: Dad you know we're broke. I'll sell this so we can get some food and you can pay my school fees.

Baba Timo (defeated): Okay then, get inside. The others are already in there.

Neighbor (laughing a little): Aha! Kids nowadays!

Baba Timo: Do you see him? He spent all weekend picking up scrap metal because the schools are closed.

Neighbor: He will become a respected member of the community, not like these ones. Do you see them? (The neighbor points to two people staggering by.) They've been given schooling but after all that effort and money, this is the result!

Baba Timo: Look at him! He's not even embarrassed to pee in the open!"

The second drunkard is urinating against the wall, not giving a damn.

A crow is perched on a broken green streetlamp and marabou storks rest on a couple acacia trees along the street, one of them hopping from here to there before limping over to a non-approved refuse pit next to the bus station. Bachelors and early risers are to blame for the piles of garbage on the street. They started by leaving a single paper bag, then the next day two paper bags. Soon everyone who got up early was doing the same with their own trash, and eventually, the garbage piled up.

Timo is scavenging for scrap metal and plastic at this dump site. He turns to his left and sees an *original* street boy approaching. Usually, the neighborhood's street kids call a boy like Timo "mbagishon," meaning a *clean* street kid.

Street boy 1: We told you that kids still in school don't do this kind of work. We told you this work is not for people like you...go back to school!

Street boy 2: But first, give that here.

Timo: No.

The street boy tries to grab Timo's collection; Timo refuses.

"Let it gooooo," the second street boy shrieks, grabbing Timo by the chin. Timo falls and the street boys run off.

After a while, the bongau—or maybe you call it a marabou stork—shits on Timo's face and the cold returns him to consciousness. He walks home, his lips slightly bleeding.

The Brookside milk vendor's bicycle bell transports him into a memory. The incident occurred when he was eleven years old, three years ago, whereas now he is fourteen years old and a candidate for the Kenya Certificate of Primary Education examinations.

Eleven-year-old Timo is leaning on the wall behind the eighth-grade classroom. The other side is caught up in celebration, with students holding their exam pads and mathematical sets. The air is full of happy voices and murmurs, the sounds of kids jumping up and down, of hugs and kisses. Everyone is celebrating the completion of the KCPE exams.

Timo joins them with a serious expression on his face.

Student 1: Look at this guy.

The murmurs die down and all attention is directed to Timo.

Student 2: Why so serious? What's the problem?

Just then another student arrives carrying a boom box on his shoulder. Attention shifts away from Timo.

Boi: Hahaha, Njoro, did you bring your speaker from home? Your head is not okay!

Njoro: Hey hey, calm down... I have a crazy mix for the end of exams.

He switches on the boom box, which lets out: "a big tuuuunnnee...," a horn blast, and then: "DJ Bunduki on the mix...the rough and roughest." This is followed by a ragga riddim, and then everyone is dancing; the girls hike up their skirts as the boys hold on to them from behind.

The same DJ mix is now blasting from a passing matatu, but it's a different crowd. There are car horns everywhere, plus cops, hawkers, brokers, hustlers, rich fellows, and Timo, who is hawking peanuts.

"Who else? Who else?" he shouts.

Suddenly, someone grabs hold of him from behind. People look on, pretending not to stare. This is just how it goes.

Stranger (angry): You fala, who told you that you could sell peanuts here?

Timo: What do you want? If you don't have money, leave me alone.

The stranger moves closer to Timo, grabs him by the shirt, and gets up in his face. Another boy joins in too, and soon, a crowd has formed around them. Someone grabs five bags of peanuts from Timo's stash and points at him, saying: "You fala, this is our territory."

Timo: You're the fala. Give me the money for the peanuts, and don't think we're friends. I don't want any trouble.

Then a heavy fist finds Timo, followed by a headlock. The peanuts fly into the air and Timo can't tell whether he's seeing nuts or stars. Trouble!

Baba Timo is holding his newspaper, waiting for food to be served, as Mama Timo enters from the other corner of the room, carrying a plate of tilapia and ugali. As usual, the food is placed on the table and Timo's brother and sister salivate, eager to dig in.

Baba Timo: Every day it's fish and ugali, fish and ugali. What have the neighbors been teaching you?

Mama Timo: In fact, fish is in very high demand right now. Why don't you find some money and start a fish business so you can stop looking for a job? Don't you know there is no work, Baba?

Baba Timo: Where is the money for that? Mother-of-my-children, Timo is supposed to join form one.

Mama Timo: Father-of-my-children, won't the NGO people pay the fees?

Baba Timo: They pay eighty percent. We pay twenty percent and we buy the uniform!

Mama Timo: Don't worry. God will come through for us.

Baba Timo has three children: two boys and a small girl. There are five years between Timo and Toni. Timo is fifteen years old now and ready to join form one. His parents are proud of his hard work, especially when, after the KCPE exams, Timo became a young hawker in Nairobi. It was this kind of hard work that had attracted Mama Timo to Baba Timo, but nowadays Mama Timo is weary of her husband because he's become lazy. He lost his job five years ago and became an alcoholic, abandoning all ambition or resolve to look for work. Baba Timo is still in denial; he lives in a world of pipe dreams, convinced it won't be long until he returns to his job at Samken Logistics as a machine operator. Mama Timo has gotten tired of his version of the events that led to him being fired. According to Baba Timo, someone had bewitched him, and his workmates had thrown juju at him. But the reality was that companies were streamlining their workers in response to the economic downturn.

And so, for years now Mama Timo has been the sole breadwinner. She sells secondhand clothes at Gikomba Market, and she is proud of her son Timo's recent contributions from his peanut-hawking business. How she wishes his twin were still around. She regrets having given one of the twins up for adoption, but she'd had no choice—they'd been broke and jobless fifteen years ago. Back then, they'd lived in the Koch shanties, in a mud house with drum roofing. Though it isn't much better, now they live in a stone-house plot and share a toilet with seven other people. Visiting the bathroom in the morning is a way to meet your neighbors because everyone uses the bathroom in turns. This is how they all know the guy who leaves the place foul; you don't want to go in there after him. This is also where people bathe, as well as a meeting place for secret lovers. The sink is here too; all the amenities are communal and located at the end of the plot.

Every plot has its secrets: Who is trying to get with whom? Who beats their wife every night, who's a drunk, who has been saved? Most Fridays, there is a Christian crusade as church members troop to Mama Timo's for prayers. Baba Timo makes himself scarce and spends his evening at Kahuruko bar instead, drinking barley with his fellow oldies, all of them telling similar stories about how they once had money before the devil materialized in their lives.

Baba Timo's family lives in a single room with a curtain that splits it in two. Timo sleeps on the sofa and the other two children sleep on a cloth spread out for them on the floor. For the last three years, Mama Timo has retreated from their sex life, telling herself it is because Timo has become a young adolescent. But the truth is that ever since Baba Timo started drinking, he has become a one-minute man, and Mama Timo is often left hanging. But no matter—she's already sorted herself out with the neighbor's husband, and so that is how they live.

For his part, Baba Timo gets his services from a Kahuruko barmaid. Mama Timo's friends gossip that Baba Timo is the one paying for the barmaid Waithera's house, but after Baba Timo slapped his wife for going to make enquiries there three years ago, she shut up about it. She found herself a side piece instead, though she feels guilty about it every day, afraid her children will find out.

Oftentimes kids reveal love scandals through their innocent

teasing. "You better shut up...your mother comes to our house to eat our food when our mother is not around," a neighbor's son told Timo once four years ago, but luckily no one was in the plot to understand what he'd let slip.

Timo wakes up in a confused state. He picks up his peanuts and puts them back in the basin, but most of them have already been stolen. Suddenly, a city council askari appears and kicks Timo with his boots.

Askari: You, nyang'au, what are you doing here? Quit clowning around.

"I was attacked by thieves," Timo defends himself.

Askari: What thieves? Get up and go home. Unless you want me to throw you in the truck...I don't care if you're just a small child.

The askari slaps him on the back. Timo forgets about his peanuts and disappears. He has heard stories of people getting locked up for hawking. He takes River Road so that he can go down to OTC bus station and board a matatu. A couple of minutes later, when he's only about a hundred meters from his matatu station, he is startled by the sound of people screaming. Then come the loud bangs of metal doors slamming shut and the beeping of car horns, as smoke fills the air. It doesn't take long for Timo to realize it's tear gas. He darts down a different alleyway. He can't see very well. Everyone is in save–yourself mode. From time to time, he bumps into someone else, but it is every man for himself.

Assailed by uncertainty, people are running left and right, but Timo slows down.

Along the side of the road a man is splayed out on the ground. In rapid succession, passersby slow down, stand for a moment by his side, then keep on running. Blood is flowing from the man's leg. Timo, momentarily stunned by the sight, returns to his senses and runs toward a matatu. Once on board, he takes a seat next to an old man and tries to calm down.

"Was that man back there a thief?" the old man asks.

"I don't know," Timo answers.

"Is he dead?" another voice inquires.

"I think so," Timo answers, breathing heavily.

"I say let the thieves die! They're the ones terrorizing us at night," a young woman's voice contributes from the back seat.

"What did he steal?" the woman in the front seat asks.

"Apparently a loaf of bread," comes an old man's voice from the back.

"Stop your malice," cries another woman, her voice full of bitterness and compassion. "I saw it with my own eyes. He was a hawker! Sold me a piece of cloth a few minutes before the city council askaris beat him up! That man was not a thief."

More conversations spring up, and soon everyone delivers their own account of the events. Even the drunks contribute. When they grow tired of talking, the bus falls silent, and before long, music comes on over the speakers.

The atmosphere on the bus shifts. The seats on this matatu are velvet, and its inner walls are covered in graffiti and posters of black American stars glaring out at us as if we still had beef between us!

...Noma, noma...noma... A ragga riddim is blasting from the speakers and the passengers' eyes are glued to the plasma screen showing palm trees against a backdrop of aqua-blue skies. Jamaican musicians are the main attraction, but there's also a sideshow of scantily dressed women in bikinis. It's impossible to daydream in a matatu; it's always braking abruptly and unexpectedly, forcing you to stay alert. You better hold onto the seat in front of you with both hands, otherwise your head may hit the ceiling. And the impact of falling back onto your seat will hurt too, especially if your buttocks don't have good shock absorbers. The drivers have no pity, plus it's not really their fault, as their schedule leaves them no alternative. It's the rat race, and on the Nairobi roads it's the drivers who call the shots. Here, breaking the rules is as normal as

blinking an eye, breaking rules *is* the rule.

"Conductor, where's your seat?" asks a cop who's just gotten on the matatu. The conductor signals something to him, the cop disembarks, and the conductor follows. Two minutes later, there's a loud bang on the matatu's body, and just like that, the matatu is back in motion.

VJ, aka DJ Kalonje, is on the steel wheels, the track comes back on where it left off, the entertainment is full blast, and after a little while, the loudspeaker gets so loud it almost blows people's hearts out.

Timo disembarks the matatu in K-Town, where it's bustling with people and evening activity: music hawkers busy with their TVs on the streets, selling CDs and DVDs; women chopping vegetables at kiosks; and the smell of fried fish and burned animal fat from all the nyama choma joints. K-Town is shrouded in heavy darkness, and murmurs abound. People get clipped by milk vendors' bicycles as they speed by delivering milk or bread, and the butchers and retail shops still have customers, but the ones doing the most business are selling mutura, liver, and bone broth, and so among the murmurs the most audible sound is the soup person, clad in a white dust coat, sloshing his soup in his jerry can.

Occasionally you'll hear screams as you walk down the streets. Most of the time they're the cries of newborns...and the stories you hear about hospitals sure are crazy. There is no medication, since all of it has been sold to the neighborhood pharmacies, and the story of the infamous Pastor Deya has only made things worse.... If you give birth at the hospital, the chances are high that your baby will mysteriously disappear.

The second scream: on the same street, a person is getting mugged...*ngeta*. The evening rush when men take home their quarter kilogram of meat after feasting with their friends is cause for celebration for K-Town's petty thieves. In most cases, the unsuspecting victims are drunk, but sometimes they are sober, and that's when things move fast. On these streets, you have to look to your left, your right, and behind you just to make sure that your ass isn't next in line. This is known as street smarts, and it includes keeping your ears open for gunshots ringing out. This is just how it is, no big deal. Although residents pay taxes to the self-appointed community police, there is a thin line separating the thieves and police.

The third scream could be anyone's. Amidst this fracas, the cops' patrol cars provide light for a while, but the residents pay for it heavily. The cars' headlights are always on full beam, the cars stand far apart, and Kiganjo's boys—or Murungaru's boys...kwekwe...spider...beasts...mambang'a, etc....the names are endless—get out of the cars and spread out, mixing with the people. So, our third scream is from a kibare, or if you don't understand, I mean a proper slap. Either a guy has been found with only twenty shillings in his pocket or a mother has come over to defend her child.

Mama: You are arresting my child for what reason? I sent him to the shops just now!

Cop (with a heavy slap: *twaafff!*): Mama, we know your child... he is a criminal. We have been tracking him for a while now.

In a scenario like this, the only option is to rush to your mattress stash, or to ask Mama Mboga Wamercy to lend you one hundred shillings to release your child. Every resident is vulnerable to transforming into a Pesa Point in that darkness. Handcuffs function just like an ATM card.

The fourth scream is lovely. After all that drama, all roads lead, of course, to the home. The plots are close together, bumper to bumper, including some of the ngoro variety, which is to say: high-rise apartments. Every apartment has approximately fifteen people, so with a ngoro you multiply, and although the entire country withstands heavy downpours, power rationing here is still as common as oxygen, and how will the rationing ever end, what with the ministers or the MPs selling power to Kayole Gen? Diesel generators are churning electricity, but according to official reports, a foreign company is still being granted the contract to ease rationing...all these years, even after La Niña and El Niño, people don't understand that rationing is over...so back to our fourth scream...

It comes after the candle-lit dinners, after watching the news of the same old boring leaders with the same old script: the Anglo Leasing scandal, the Goldenberg scandal, maize scandal, the Triton oil deals, citizen protests, and last but not least, KCC pouring out thousands of liters of milk. A ghetto queen serves food to her father, then takes her position watching South American soaps or Nigerian movies, and after that it is off to slumberland...even though in some cases it starts beforehand: the lovey-dovey stuff.

The scenario is similar on Koinange Street, but there, the "conflict" is between city officials, perverts, and thieves seeking pleasure and the thigh-land squad hustling to pay bills, raise children, and save for college fees. And don't forget Sunday morning church service...this squad might just be the biggest contributors to the coffers!

When Timo reaches home that night, the plot's main gate is not yet locked, and he enters the house at around ten.

Baba Timo: How was your day, my child?

Timo: Good, Dad.

Mama Timo (proudly): How is business?

Timo: City council officers, Mama.

The parents exchange looks, and their silence tells Timo everything. They don't need to hear the whole story, as it isn't the first time this kind of thing has happened.

Mama Timo: My child, we left you some food. Us, we're going to bed.

Baba Timo follows his wife, and the two disappear behind the curtain where their bed is.

Mama Timo: When you're done, light the mosquito coil and don't forget to turn off the lights.

Timo: Okay, Mama.

As Timo dishes up some food for himself, he's surprised to find his brother's eyes wide open.

"Hey, Toni, children your age are usually asleep by now… what are you waiting for?"

"What did you bring for us, Timo?" Toni asks in a whisper.

Mama Timo: Toni! If you are not asleep by the time I get off this bed then you will be sorry. And Timo, you should wake up early tomorrow, get the money from under the radio, go to Gikomba, and buy a metal suitcase. We are taking you to boarding school tomorrow.

Toni winks at his brother and covers himself with the blanket. Their sister, Sara, is next to him snoring, deep in slumberland. After half an hour, Timo lights the candle, switches off the lights, turns off the radio, and goes to sleep.

In the morning, K-Town is radiant, a clear sky with patches of clouds here and there, children busy going to school, the mama mbogas on their way back from the market, industrial area workers, the matatu army taking over the streets, and even people getting up early to go to work at the slaughterhouse in Dagoretti. Njiru, Kiamaiko, and Burma are also bustling with motorbikes and their red and black cars, everyone on their way, which is to say, on the streets: civil servants, doctors, lawyers, entrepreneurs, hawkers, street preachers, con artists, real artists...all of them have risen early in the name of nation building. K-Town's residents are very hardworking.

Timo gets up early and heads to the bus stop, and before long, a matatu arrives.

"*Every day I'm hustling...* This is Hepta Entertainment... DJ Mantrix on the mix," the plasma screen announces loud and clear.

Fresh perfumed air hits Timo smack in the face, and turning to his side, he sees a beautiful girl smiling.

Timo: Hey, where are you off to this early in the morning?

Girl: Who told you I wanted to talk to you?

Timo: Oohh...I'm sorry!

"I'm returning home because I'm going to school tomorrow," she says, before falling silent.

"Which school have you been assigned?" Timo asks.

She takes Timo in, from his shoes up to his face, then, reluctantly: "What's your name and what do you want?"

"Timo," he says.

"Mr. Timo, my name is Suzy, and I don't want to be bothered, okay? What time is it right now? It's too early."

Timo gives up and stares out his window. Soon the matatu has passed through Huruma, then Air Force, finally reaching Eastleigh.

Matatus and graffiti proclaiming powerful names such as Field Marshal Kimathi, Street Soldiers, Rebel, Harlem, Mafia Squad, Black Militias; street theaters, people like ants crisscrossing the street, men in kanzus, women in buibuis, girls in hip-hugger jeans, boys in hoodies.

This is the scene: the air is scented with the sweetness of biriani, plus other spices, clothing, and perfumes. Electronic shops are everywhere, and the air is abuzz with the Number

Nine buses' horns and the traders' loudspeakers. Like K-Town residents, people on this side of the city are very hardworking, and yet there is more official cartel activity here. Uncollected garbage is piled everywhere, even next to the Air Force base, and the roads are riddled with potholes.

The matatu barrels down the main road, then past Mater Hospital, Eastleigh. Past the state-of-the-art shopping malls lining both sides of the road, and then, a big mosque. The sun takes its position in the sky, and doves settle on wires, fluttering their wings.

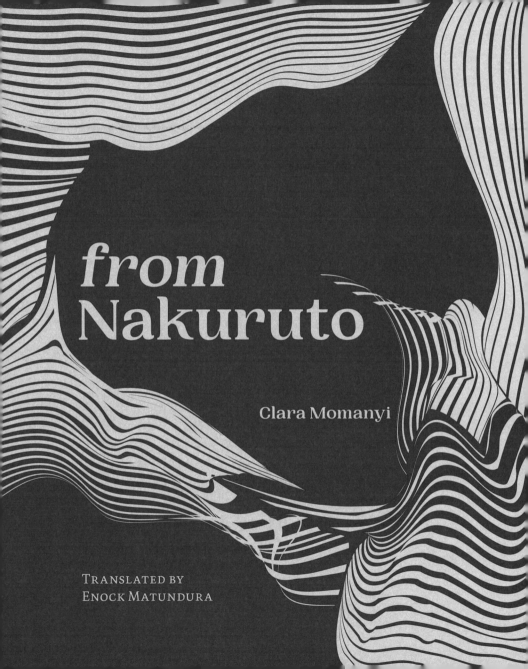

from
Nakuruto

Clara Momanyi

TRANSLATED BY
ENOCK MATUNDURA

Aliufungua mlango wa chumba
chake cha kulala, taratibu akajikokota
hadi kitandani. Alijitupa huko
kama gunia la viazi. Muda si muda,
aliingia katika ulimwengu wa ndoto.

NAKURUTO'S WHOLE BODY HURT. SHE WAS TIRED, AS IF SHE had been pushing a handcart around all day. Opening the door to her bedroom, she staggered toward her bed and threw herself down like a sack of potatoes. Almost immediately, she started dreaming. Dreams allowed her to temporarily escape the reality of everyday life, which had long exasperated her, casting her into a deep depression. She now found herself out of her element, far from the reality she had been used to. Yes, it was this reality that had made her restless, hysterical, and confused in her heart. Her bed was the only place where she could forget her troubles, even if only for a short while. She was grateful that God had created sleep for human beings. Without sleep, the world would have been full of mad people.

Having entered this sphere involuntarily, Nakuruto began exploring the dreamland. The difference between everyday life and the dreamland was that she was more comfortable in the dream, even though here she remained a spectator of events she could not control. And so, she surrendered herself to this new reality, hoping to control her emotions while rediscovering a chapter of forgotten history from long, long ago. This new reality would gradually and willingly unearth today's dreams, in addition to those chapters that had long been buried in the debris of time, making Nakuruto yearn for tomorrow. This so-called *reality* would make her divine her own future like a prophet, a prophet of her own life. First though, back in the dreamland, an unknown force suddenly took hold of Nakuruto, shaking her terribly, then lifting her off the ground. Excited, she soared like a vulture high in the sky.

Although she had no wings, Nakuruto flew at a terrific speed. She felt as though she were passing through a vacuum of total darkness; as if she were chasing time backward, to where she'd originated from; as if she were watching flashbacks in a fast-paced movie. At such a speed, you had to keep your eyes wide open so as not to miss a thing.

Suddenly, she was whizzed through what appeared to be ancient caves. The caves were opening their mouths to welcome her. Cave after cave swallowed her whole, each one bigger than the last.

She saw very strange things in those caves. Tortoise shells were scattered everywhere, as well as stones carved into various forms, some circular and oval, others cone-shaped. There were also the huge skeletons of creatures she couldn't identify; her legs, dangling in the air like those of a bird in flight, struck the bones as she passed. She also saw gigantic, coiled snakes resembling multicolored head wraps. Scared stiff at the sight of them, she began trembling like grass in a storm. Next appeared a group of small creatures, half-human, half-animal, huddled together as though warming themselves around a fire. They stared up at her, looks of disappointment on their faces. Nakuruto closed her eyes; the creatures made her anxious. When she opened them again, she saw paintings of animals on the walls of the caves, including a large ape. The animals looked scary. Eyes protruding, they seemed ready to pounce on Nakuruto at any moment for intruding into their territory. She was now flying over the half-buried fossils of early humans, and she squeezed her eyes shut again.

Nakuruto kept her eyes closed as she passed over the debris of collapsed structures where those animals depicted in the cave paintings had once lived. Then, abruptly and inexplicably, her eyes were forced back open. She tried to shut them again to avoid seeing the unfolding magic tricks, but in vain. The force propelling her through the old ruins was now keeping her eyes open, compelling her to look at what she did not want to see. She tried to lift her hand to cover her face, but it was as heavy as an anchor. It was then that Nakuruto realized she had no choice but to confront this new reality, though it made her tremble as if she had malaria. She had no choice but to come to terms with the unfolding curtains of history. For history is an indelible reality, one that is shaped in the minds of humans through narratives, understood through neither critical thinking nor logic. But whatever that was unfolding in front of her was quite different. It was some kind of reality that could not be deciphered using dream logic. She believed that a reality founded on historical facts would never be ignored.

Wafting through the air, Nakuruto tried to pinch herself to ascertain whether she was indeed dreaming or not, but each time she tried, she found that her hand was too heavy to lift. So, she remained suspended in the air, her mouth agape in shock. After a while, she was able to look around her once more, glancing at the stone carvings, as well as some strange paraphernalia, undoubtedly used by those creatures of yore. Then, Nakuruto was led through the oval entrance of a massive cave.

The cave was empty. Ahead of her shone a piercing ray of glittering light that caused tears to flow freely from her eyes. Whisked through the cave at a terrific speed, Nakuruto reached the far end and was thrust out through another oval opening. In front of her was a dense forest and tall, snow-capped mountains. The glittering snow was captivating, and for the first time on this journey, she found herself smiling. Rivulets of water were cascading down the mountainsides and into the forest, forming springs of water that glittered in the sun, while birds flew by overhead, seeming to bask in the beauty all around them. Even though Nakuruto was barreling through the forest at such a high speed, she did note that the trees were larger than any she had seen before in her entire life.

These trees were home to all kinds of animals. There were chimpanzees, monkeys, hartebeest, giraffes, rhinos, buffalos, elephants, leopards, wild boars, and other, smaller animals such as warthogs, hares, mongooses, porcupines, and even beavers.

Small black monkeys jumped from tree to tree, their young ones hanging from their waists, and made noises to express their happiness and satisfaction. Birds of all varieties flew from one branch to another up in the treetops, while others built nests to safeguard their young. Some trees bent under the weight of ripe fruit. However, what most amazed Nakuruto was the harmonious way the animals lived together in that paradise. There wasn't an iota of enmity among them. They all ate together. There was no sign of hostility anywhere.

After the forest, the force propelled her through a vast desert that seemed completely devoid of life, the ground cracked from the heat. "Ah! Is this not hell?" she cried out.

"Poor me, I have been thrust from the frying pan into the fire." Nakuruto felt the urge to speak aloud to herself as she flew higher up in the sky. But at that moment, she collided with a dust storm. She was afraid she would be blinded by the hot grains of sand and dust now battering her entire body, but luckily not a single particle entered her eyes. She wondered whether the creatures she had seen earlier in the forest were alive or just fossils, like those she had seen in the caves. Suddenly, a huge creature was blown toward her in a cloud of dust, striking her hard in the ribs. She opened her mouth to scream, but no sound came out.

"Oh my God! I am in hell for sure. I am burning alive!" she thought to herself. Still, Nakuruto had no choice but to leave her destiny in the hands of the force that was propelling her onward. She had become a slave to the force. She was moving faster now and having trouble breathing. She tried to shut her eyes again, without success. The speed was making her feel dizzy, and she couldn't hear anything anymore. She was flung up, down, and side-to-side like a piece of paper caught in a ferocious whirlwind. Her heart was beating hard, loud, and constant like a drum. My goodness, where is she being taken now?

Frightened, Nakuruto beseeched God to save her from the unfathomable force. She passed through a series of curtains; as soon as she passed through one, another one opened, on and on into its vacuous depths, disorienting her even further. At her current speed, she had no time to explore anything. Everything was passing in a blur from one curtain to another. All of a sudden, the scenery changed again, as she was transported from the desert into a savanna, reviving her hopes. The cool breeze thrilled her, although she knew she was not out of the woods yet. From a distance, Nakuruto could see a pack of animals big and small. There wasn't a single human being in sight. The animals were grazing together in perfect harmony. A lioness was breastfeeding a gazelle fawn, and a hyena was feeding together with a young hartebeest. These two incidents astounded her. She thought perhaps she was on another planet, having left Earth altogether.

The savanna had tall grass and winding rivers, whose waters flowed into the unknown. Sometimes, the rivers seemed to be asking to be shown the way; other times, it was as if they were arguing after realizing they had been misled. Slowing down now, Nakuruto was able to see the landscape more clearly. Ahead of her, she saw tremendous, exciting changes, including trees and other flora that she could recognize. On the horizon, groups of animals resembling cows were being herded by a human figure. The strange force eventually brought Nakuruto low enough to see herds of sheep, goats, and calves grazing.

Here too were herdsmen wearing loincloths, water gourds slung on leather straps around their necks. Bows rested on their shoulders and quivers of arrows hung on their backs. She was frightened by the way they were standing, ready to shoot anyone they deemed threatening. Nakuruto prayed that the force would not drop her down there. Those weapons were surely a sign of the herders' hostility. Indeed, she was in a hostile environment. Here, the lion did not feed together with the sheep or goats, and the gazelles did not share anything as she had seen them do earlier. The animals had distinct and clear boundaries. What had caused such enmity? Nakuruto couldn't say. It puzzled her. Perhaps the answer lay somewhere in the events that were unfolding in front of her with the passage of time. Could it be that the journey she was on could also help her solve this riddle?

Still lost in thought, Nakuruto began descending so quickly that she felt like vomiting. Her legs dangled in the air as she let the force carry her wherever it wanted. Her stomach ached and started swelling slowly. Her skin was crawling, as though covered by millions of spiders. She had no choice but to give in to the force. She was a weak creature, unable even to blink her eyes, let alone shut her mouth. Her throat was dry and sore from swallowing so much air. Eventually, the force dropped her to the ground with a thud!

The crash changed Nakuruto completely. She lay there where she had fallen, finally able to blink her eyes and close her mouth, but her lips were raw and peeling from the wind. Her body felt heavy, and she gasped for air like an asthmatic patient. Without doubt, Nakuruto was exhausted. She lay there silently, resting right where she had fallen, listening to her heart beating like a drum in her chest. She tried to turn over, but she felt pain everywhere. What shocked her most, however, were her hands. They were withered like the back of a tree. Her skin, badly bruised, sagged with wrinkles as if she were an old person. Her veins were visible through the skin. They too looked warped, tangled like a web or a net used to catch sardines.

"Poor me! Have I become old?" She had regained her voice. She was yelling as though face-to-face with the devil himself.

"Is this me or someone else?" she wondered, trying to stand up. She felt weak like before. She lifted herself with difficulty, her legs wobbling like those of an old woman. She touched her head. Alas! Her smooth hair had become rough, like a swarm of houseflies circling her head.

"This can't be true! This is a dream, I am dreaming. I must be in dreamland. Dreams can sometimes bring about sorcery. No, this can't be me." She pinched herself to ensure that she was not dreaming and felt pain.

"No! So, this is real. Was it the same force that whisked me here that made me old?" she asked herself, disappointed. The more changes she noticed in her body and worldview, the more her mind matured. Nakuruto now felt like someone who had lived a long life. It dawned on her that her life experience had endowed her with the wisdom and visions of old age, which indeed made her an old woman. At her feet lay an old basket woven from palm leaves, blackened with age. Inside were a scrap of old, black fabric from the kind of wrap worn by old women, plus a hoe, a handleless knife, and a small gourd filled with water.

"Nakuruto, these are the possessions of an old person," she told herself. "Therefore, you must be an old woman, one who lived just as you are living right now." And the longer she gazed at the basket, the more clues were revealed about where she had come from.

Beside the old basket was a long, black walking stick. Nakuruto examined her body keenly. The palms of her hands were riddled with blisters, a sign of backbreaking work. Her fingernails were hard and blackened like those of a root digger. She wore bangles on her wrists and a necklace around her neck. An old, black wrap covered her chest, and another was tied around her waist. Her legs were dirty and swollen as though bitten by an army of insects. Her skin looked faded from a lack of care. Coming to terms with the ways time had taken its toll on her body, she bent over with difficulty and picked up her walking stick. Her hands trembled, a symptom of age, hunger, and fatigue. Supporting herself with the walking stick, she stood there thinking for a while, casting her eyes ahead. In the distance were three neighboring villages, each with a fence of tree branches around its perimeter, the gate made from pieces of lumber clamped together. Off in the distance, animal noises mixed with the calls of the people herding them.

The mid-afternoon sun beat down on Nakuruto, blurring her vision. She bent once more with difficulty and picked up the basket, then opened the gourd and drank greedily to quench her thirst. The heat made her legs heavy as she slowly made her way toward the three villages. The earth was dry beneath her feet, and with each step she left behind a cloud of dust, which in turn only made her hotter. She started sweating profusely. To protect her legs, she walked in the grass alongside the path leading to the villages. However, her journey was interrupted by burrs from creeping grass, which forced her now and again to bend with difficulty to pluck them from her feet.

As she walked, Nakuruto talked to herself: "People have forgotten the traditions that used to guide their lives. They have ignored the sacred rules and behaved unnaturally. They have rejected the ways of our ancestors and done away with the old sacrifices. They have abandoned the paths—now filled with weeds—and are lost. And there they remain, lost in the dark, with nothing to hold on to," These utterances left her mouth in one continuous breath, and she took the first step on her journey looking for the lost way.

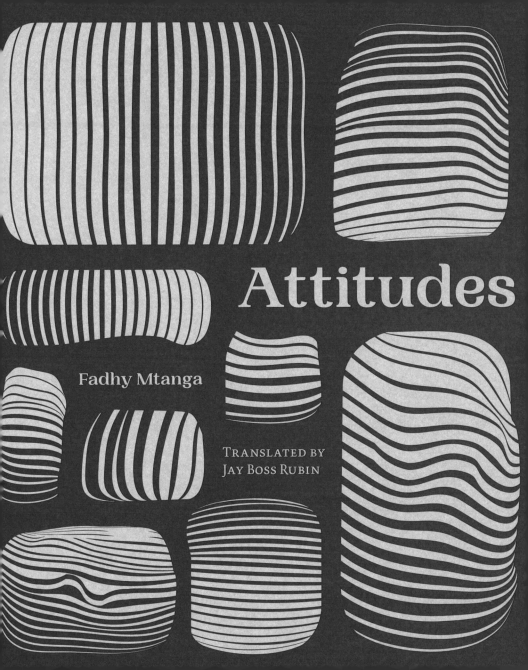

Attitudes

Fadhy Mtanga

Translated by
Jay Boss Rubin

Alipomwona mtu wa siti ya
mbele yake akihangaika kuziba
pua, na sekunde chache tu
jirani yake, na jirani yake, soni
ilimvavagaa kibati.

"I BEG YOUR PARDON, CHILD—MAY I PLEASE PASS?"

"Hold on," Nela said. The woman standing beside her, asking to pass, was about twice her age. Right away, Nela regretted looking the woman up and down as she answered her.

"C'mon, let's go," instructed the mpigadebe from the bus stand in Ipogoro. Someone was clogging up the corridor. "Oyaa," he said forcefully. "Scoot to the side, you're jamming up the aisle."

"My daughter," implored the middle-aged woman a second time, "Let me pass so those behind me can pass, too." She couldn't understand what the girl was doing, shuffling her luggage around in the overhead carrier when people were trying to squeeze by.

"Hey," Nela raised her voice. "Didn't I tell you to wait?"

The woman didn't mind waiting, actually. But the passengers behind her were starting to pile up and press against her—she was beginning to feel crushed, overwhelmed. What was this girl doing still messing around with her suitcases? The woman had to ease the tension somehow before the mpigadebe blew his lid. She was all too familiar with the notoriously short fuses of station agents, and today she couldn't risk a misunderstanding. She didn't want to be bothered at all, in fact. Her nerves were still jangled from the news she'd received earlier, and she had more than enough on her mind. Her son, who worked for the municipal council in Morogoro, had been accused of misplacing a few million of the city's shillings. She'd run out the door the moment she learned of the scandal and hadn't even had a moment to catch her breath. To avoid being caught in the flare-up she feared was about to erupt, she slipped into the nearest row that had an open space.

"Mama," Nela addressed her right away. "You're sitting in my seat."

"Forgive me, my child," the woman explained. "I thought if I could squeeze in for just a moment…"

"But didn't I tell you to wait?" Nela shouted, exasperated.

A passenger seated in the row behind them couldn't resist weighing in—she was compelled to, in a way, by her sense of civic duty. She didn't like how the interaction had played out; it didn't sit well with her; plus, she had already decided on the best way to present the case. "Dada," she began, "you were blocking the aisle, were you not? How long did you expect this poor woman to wait?"

Nela didn't hesitate. "Was I talking to you?"

"Where's your sense of decency?" this other passenger asked, appealing now to her bus full of jurors. She didn't give Nela the opportunity to respond. "This woman is old enough to be your mother. Why couldn't you have just let her pass?"

"Please," Nela insisted. "It's got nothing to do with you."

"Today's women," another passenger observed, "give a whole new meaning to the word *shida*."

He'd only intended to share his observation with his friend in the next seat, but his whispered words reached Nela before they could dissipate. "Listen mzee," she shot back, "how about you mind your own business?"

"I wasn't talking to you," the man responded. He wasn't merely putting on a show for his fellow passengers—to him, the situation wasn't a funny one. "It's you, young lady, who had better *mind* something," he clarified. "Mind your tongue, at once!"

Nela backed down. As she quieted, the other passengers' jeers echoed in her ears. "Jamani," she pleaded. "I let her pass, what else do you want from me?"

Most of the passengers saw in Nela a sloppily dressed, insolent brat. Three seats away, though, sat a passenger named

Sowa who saw a pretty young thing whose clothes gripped her body. Her forest-green shorts stopped above her knees, revealing about a quarter of her ample thighs. The dark fabric contrasted nicely with her light skin. Below her thighs were plump, sumptuous calves, and above them was a big, beautiful bundle of a behind. She had perfect proportions, he thought, and was just the right height: neither short nor tall. Her hair looked good, too. Rows met at right angles at the back of her head and around the sides, and converged in a small, pompadour-like kiduku hump. The work of a talented stylist, no doubt. Sowa couldn't stop staring. All he could think about was how to score Nela's number.

While Sowa mulled over his strategy, the bus kept barreling along toward Dar es Salaam, the biggest city in all of East Africa. The atmosphere within the coach was as lively and cacophonous as their destination, but the travelers' voices couldn't compete with the onboard TV monitors, which were blasting Tanzanian comedies. Some passengers tried to sleep, slumped against their chairs. Others chattered with their neighbors. Others were silent, lost in swirling thought.

Nela was among this last group. They had left from Iringa less than an hour ago and had not yet reached even Ilula when an unsettled feeling suddenly rose up in her. She didn't understand what it was, but she felt it most of all in her stomach.

Fadhy Mtanga

Her insides tensed up all at once, as if she'd just set foot inside Kariakoo, Dar es Salaam's largest, most chaotic market. At first, Nela thought she just needed to fart. But something warned her, don't you dare.

As the bus picked up speed, a steady drizzle began to fall. It was January, and new growth peppered the landscape as far as the eye could see. The ever-changing picture out the window was a pleasant one: mountains and hills rolling along with the road. The passengers who opened their eyes to their surroundings weren't disappointed.

Sowa gazed out the window, but he didn't soak up any of the scenery. He was thinking only of the female passenger who, abruptly and without warning, had taken prisoner of his heart.

Nela was still feeling uneasy. People were doing little somersaults inside her stomach. A whole dance party was popping off in there; she had to do something to ease the pressure. She shifted side to side, letting out little puffs of gas. It was exhausting. She didn't know how much longer she could tolerate the contents of her stomach dancing the amapiano. Did it smell, too? It is what it is, she told herself.

Carefully, so her neighbor would neither notice nor tender a guess, Nela leaned up on one butt cheek again. Midway through a long gust of flatulence, her control started to slip.

Nela reversed course—she tried as hard as she could to hold everything in. Sweat poured from her body; her torso began to shake. Then she felt the wetness where she was sitting and knew it was all over—everything was ruined.

She sat still for a few seconds, trying to assess what to do. The person in the seat in front of her was the first to cover their nose, then passengers in adjacent seats started covering their noses, too. Disgust rolled forward like a wave, and right behind it, filling the entire bus, was Nela's shame. Her seat felt even wetter than it had been before. An awful, acrid smell invaded her nostrils.

"Brother, excuse me," Nela said to the passenger next to her. She didn't care that she hadn't returned the man's greeting when they'd taken their seats that morning. After a hasty brainstorming session, Nela concluded she had no other option than to ask for his help.

The man, who was youngish, hesitated. He wasn't sure that she was really speaking to him. Wasn't this the same person who'd remained silent when he'd wished her a good morning? Maybe she felt bad about it. But he couldn't ponder her situation too deeply; an unpleasant smell had been bothering him for a few minutes already. He knew what it was, but he didn't know where it was coming from.

"Brother," Nela said.

The passenger turned to face his fellow traveler, certain now that she was addressing him. He was also certain about the source of the smell. He didn't know, though, what exactly had caused it. "Naam," he responded. "You called?"

"Sorry, brother," Nela said, her voice calm but so, so timid. "I've got a little problem, you see, and I was wondering if you could assist me."

"What kind of problem, sister?"

"Stomach trouble," Nela said. She felt her face fold in on itself. "Could you ask the driver to pull over so I can relieve myself?"

He didn't need to be asked twice. The man jumped out of his seat and moved swiftly up the aisle. "Samahani, bro."

"What's up?" the driver asked, hand on the gearshift.

"If you wouldn't mind pulling over," said the man conveying the message, "there's a girl back there who really has to go."

"Tell her to hold it in. The next rest stop is Al Jazeerah."

"I don't think it can wait," the man explained. "Actually, it's already kind of too late."

"Ooh!" The driver didn't say another word. He flipped on his turn signal and, before long, the bus came to a stop on the shoulder.

"Oyaa sister. Let's get a move on. Chop chop!"

Nela couldn't budge. She felt frozen. A channel of tears flowed down each of her cheeks. Her heart was beating hard against her chest, less like an organ delivering blood and more like a bullet-spraying gun.

"Oyaa," the conductor said again as he walked toward her down the aisle. "Let's get a move on before we get left in the dust."

Nela kept crying. Not because of her upset stomach but because everything was spoiled, ruined.

"My child, can I lend you a kanga?" offered a woman seated toward the middle of the bus. She could tell this girl was not alright.

Nela nodded.

"Oyaa, what gives?" the conductor said again.

The man who had gone and asked the driver to pull over returned to his seat. Everyone scooted aside for him, making room.

"Jamani," the woman who had offered the kanga implored the rest of the bus. "Everyone back to their seats, please. Now," she insisted. "This is an emergency."

Nela accepted the kanga but didn't feel any less crushed. Her embarrassment was as heavy as the giant sacks women haul to market on their backs.

The woman positioned herself between seats, so passengers wouldn't be tempted to pry and Nela could adjust herself in private. "Wrap it around your waist as you start to stand up," she instructed.

Nela did as she was told, but all the while her sobs grew louder and louder.

"Don't cry, dear," a passenger nearby tried to comfort her.

"I'm so sorry," the woman with the kanga echoed as she helped Nela up. From her bag, she whipped out another piece of bright fabric and wiped up the yellow liquid that had pooled on Nela's seat. "C'mon, let's get off."

As Nela made her way to the front of the bus, a sharp stench accosted everyone she passed. Some held their palms up over their noses. Some buried their faces in the folds of their clothes. Others opened their windows and spat.

"Don't cry, love," the woman escorting Nela said as they stepped off. "Do you have something you can change into?"

"Yes," said Nela. This was the most mortified she'd been in years. "My bag is the red one in the overhead carrier."

The woman with the kangas asked another woman, who'd come along to assist, to go back onto the bus and retrieve Nela's suitcase.

"Please try to find my wet wipes," Nela begged. She was completely vulnerable now, naked.

Nela cleaned herself under cover of some brush off to the side of the road. She never wanted to see her soiled clothes again. She hurled them into the bushes and put on a long dress and head scarf. When she reboarded the bus, she looked like the shyest, gentlest girl in the world. Nela imagined the other passengers scratching their heads and wondering, was this the same rude girl they'd witnessed earlier, or someone new?

"People these days have a hard time holding it in."

Another voice responded softly. "Bro—she was bursting at the seams. It was only a matter of time until her brake lines blew."

The words pierced through Nela, but she couldn't summon the courage to turn and face the men who had uttered them. She was too pained. Nela had never felt so small, so invisible. For the rest of the ride, she vowed, she'd keep quiet. She'd be absolutely silent, she decided, all the way to Dar es Salaam. The bus gathered speed. They were trying to make up for the time they'd lost, most likely, when she got off to change her clothes.

Nela sank deeper and deeper into her own thoughts. The trouble was this: because no one had taught her, she had no one to blame. That's what had led her to the state she was in. Other than what she'd gleaned from watching TV (what she'd seen in secret, and with great delight), no one had bothered to teach her anything. Even setting aside this current predicament, which had snuck up on her, ambushed her, really, she'd already experienced so much misfortune.

But now, yes—that's just how life goes.

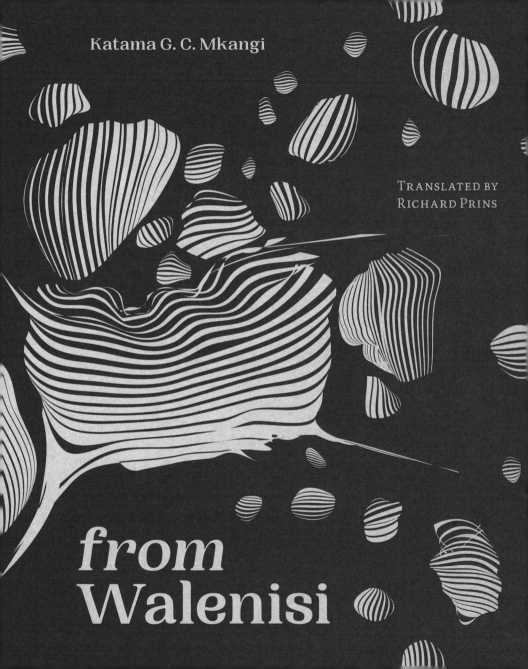

Katama G. C. Mkangi

TRANSLATED BY
RICHARD PRINS

from
Walenisi

Alikuwa si wetu tena alipotoka nje ya
nguvu za mvutano wa dunia. Huko ndani,
alitanabahi kwamba dunia ameshaiacha
milele aliposikia *Sayari* ikijinasua kwa
nguvu kwa kutengana na mvutano huo.
Kujinasua kwa *Sayari* kulikuwa kama
vile mtoto apasuavyo mimba ili naye awe
kiumbe huru kamili.

DZOMBO WASN'T EXPECTING ANY SYMPATHY FROM THE judge. Where he came from, it was understood that judges' decisions came not from their hearts, but from a place of perpetual self-interest. Just earlier that day, Dzombo had been hauled off, like some miscreant who'd leaped out of nowhere and deliberately spilled everybody's flour—so where could he expect to find any sympathy? Once you've thrown a dog a bone, it will never let you snatch it away. And if a dog can protect its own interests, why not a judge? Judges aren't dogs, they're humans!

The judge strode into the court like an angel of death. As soon as he entered, everyone was ordered to take a seat. The judge propped his bifocals on the end of his nose and, looking at Dzombo through the part that was clearest, ordered him to stand. In those days, courts had no laws pertaining to the protection, defense, or upholding of human rights. Their only job was convicting anyone who had the misfortune of being accused. So no, Dzombo wasn't expecting sympathy, but he was thunderstruck, baffled, by the sentence he was given. The judge stood up and ruled without a moment's hesitation: "Death!" Having dispensed justice, he gathered up his robes and headed for his chambers.

He left Dzombo's loved ones wailing and shouting in his wake: "Salala! Uuuiii!" While his relatives convulsed with grief, Dzombo was shunted off and dumped into a paddy wagon. Everyone present knew where the vehicle was headed. In order to see the judgment fulfilled, or else to say their last goodbyes, they exited the courtroom and resumed their grieving outside.

*

People had already crowded around the Sayari launch pad. The throng was silent, eager to witness the execution of the death sentence. This spectacle had become almost routine for them, but they weren't tired of it yet. They gathered like a herd of cows waiting to be slaughtered. Even as her friends drop dead around her, no cow believes the knife will ever come for her until the moment she feels, in the name of Allah, her own neck being slit. Ordinarily, her writhing is not associated with any intellectual complexity. After all, if cows were intellectuals, then why would we eat their meat?

Dzombo's relatives were standing as close as they could to Sayari, hoping to say one last farewell. Though they shed tears and sniffled, their grief was otherwise silent. Before them loomed the vessel of death. Sayari and its engines were thrumming, steam billowing out and flames blazing. They could hear the buzzing of an electrical current and see the exertions of the engines in the tremoring of its metal frame. The exterior sheets of white, corrugated iron, together with the large tanks of gasoline tucked under its armpit, produced a spectacular image.

This didn't have to be a death ship, his relatives were thinking. It was a vessel for traversing the sky so people could feel free. A freedom with no limit. It hadn't been intended for annihilation, but rather for research—and since when did research beget death?

Sayari hadn't built itself. Nor did it employ itself. It was built according to intensive research and development with the goal of rendering ignorance a thing of the past. It was built to discover the secrets of creation. The nature of creation is to hide; that of humanity, to expose. Sayari was an illustration of this conflict. While creation is quite pleased to have its secrets discovered, it offers no opinion as to how the fruits of this endless conflict should be put to use. This has been left to humans themselves. What brings death, and what brings life. All this is in their hands.

Sayari was just a ship. As such, it was an instrument of human self-interest. But humans tend to be most interested in deluding themselves, especially when their interests are stratified. And Sayari was awarded the job of delusion, according to this principle.

The Sayari now waiting to be launched could have been a ship of joy, rather than lamentation. It could have transported young folks to study outer space and behold an endless horizon, a projection of the youthful veins pulsing in their idealistic hearts. Or it could have taken patriots on one last sightseeing tour as they enjoyed the sunset of their lives—rather than relegating them to a thankless senility.

What bliss and ululation there would be if it could launch newlyweds on a genuinely bittersweet honeymoon! For there, they would discover the rapture of two becoming one and celebrate a feast of passion, souls fusing while bodies floated. Or as the case may be, shouting in each other's faces, caught up within a storm of loathing.

But today, Sayari had been charged with the task of human beastliness. It was just a ship, after all, and it had no choice but to go wherever it was directed. All it required was a command, that's it.

*

Dzombo was brought out once he was dressed and ready. Before this day, he had heard about "Death by Sayari," but never processed its meaning. Now the sacrificial offering was none other than himself.

"Prisoners have rights, too." Thus spoke the executioner, his voice buzzing in everyone's ears. He was telling the crowd that it was his first day on the job. And like any legitimate hangman who took pride in his work, he said, "According to the law and the civilized nature of our country, it behooves us not to deny his rights in the execution of this sentence." No further explanation was required; everyone present, including Dzombo, knew these rights well.

The first was that the condemned man could teach himself how to operate the vehicle, for a period not to exceed five minutes. The second concerned the fuel. The truth was that those tanks could only carry a certain amount. So even if the condemned man succeeded in flying it, he would have to find a place to land before the fuel ran out and Sayari dropped like a stone. Moreover, it depleted very quickly, on account of having to dodge all the asteroids scattered about in outer space. Many perished because the gas ran out while dodging these rocks; others simply collided with them.

"We have emerged from barbarism," the executioner continued. "That's why our ruler doesn't wish to kill people brutally like other rulers do. These rights give the condemned a chance to reform himself."

He was cut off by the dissatisfied murmurs of the crowd. He turned at once to Dzombo and shouted, "Dzombo, death is death and there is no coming back. These rights are the rights of death, and this Sayari is just a coffin. No one has ever returned to tell us about it—or else it wouldn't be death!" He put a self-important stress on these last words to show he was tough. And, just to spook the crowd a little more, he ended with a bang. "So come on in and die!"

Having finished, he opened Sayari's hatch. It was dark inside except for the light gleaming from a little lamp on the wall. People tried to peek inside, but they weren't able to see much, for the executioner slammed the door shut with a sudden fury. This caused an outcry of anguish, spoiling the veneer of serenity created for the ruler's entertainment. The cries came from Dzombo's supporters and relatives. Once the hatch had shut, they knew that they would never see him again. Even worse, he was being buried before he had even died, and thus his grave would never be seen by anyone... Rulers, they do have their wisdom!

Not everyone was grieving the blood of Dzombo. Many

began to disperse without contemplating what they had witnessed. As far as they were concerned, Dzombo was just unlucky. But they, they were the lucky ones; such a horror would never afflict them.

Others were delighted by the deed. They could be heard talking amongst themselves. "That's the best remedy for talking too much."

"Absolutely!" one of them replied, and added, "Now let him talk his own ear off, all alone in there!"

Another inserted himself, "He'll learn that not even the devil himself lets people run their mouths."

"But what happens if he won't keep his mouth shut?" the second one wondered anxiously.

He was answered by the first one. "Most likely, Satan will turn up with his own Sayari. If he doesn't watch out, he'll be sent to an even hotter hell!"

"Ehh! So it never ends!"

"What never ends?"

"These gates of hell," the nervous one clarified.

"You got that right. Especially for these too-much-talkers," the knowledgeable one explained. "But that's not for lucky guys like you and me."

The first one, not to be outdone, said, "All that talk is a one-way ticket to hell. It's inevitable that they wind up in the Sayari."

"So there's no need to pity anyone like them," the knower swore.

"But...what was all his talk?" the confused one asked his fellows. "Does anyone know what he actually said?"

All he got in response were blank stares, putting an end to his questions.

*

Inside the vessel, where he had been imprisoned, Dzombo was greeted by the voice of a person-machine, which informed him: "You have exactly five minutes...examine the navigation instructions in front of you...when the light turns purple, Sayari will be preparing for blastoff."

Inside his own grave, he wasted no time. Five minutes was more than enough time for a person to be resurrected—not to mention die! It was best to go out fighting. This was his position: *Where there is life, death tends to fold.*

In the dim light, he managed to read the instructions in front of him. He understood that, if he wanted to live, anger would be his greatest enemy. The important thing was to decide what was most important, so that he could learn it, then do it, and get himself to the next level.

The instructions listed the various steering functions. He was able to condense them quickly and pick the five he saw as most important. These were *ascend, cruise, dodge, dive,* and *land.* That was how he would save himself. So the next thing he did was examine the controls. He gripped the wheel and noticed it was fixed in place. He tugged, but it would not budge an inch. It was following its own orders.

This just goes to show that not everyone who calls themselves a captain has any actual authority over a steering wheel! These are fake captains. They are perfectly delighted to be called captains, even though they have no idea where the steering wheel is even located. Their ships are taken hostage and plundered by the real captains, who hide behind the scenes, treating the fake captains as their puppets, moored wherever they are told. And if they fail to follow instructions, then they find themselves flung over cliffs or trapped under avalanches, howling, stranded. Their ships crash and explode, and the real captains immediately relieve the dummy captains, replacing them with new puppets. Usually, these vicissitudes don't interfere in the slightest with the journey, which proceeds according to the whims of the real captains, always lurking behind the scenes.

Dzombo knew that if he wanted to survive, he had no choice but to grab the wheel and control it. What, again, was the meaning of having a life in your hands? Your friend has his own life, but what if your life winds up in his hands? Will he forget about his own? Dzombo was working this out in his mind. Whoever is granted such power, their own life will always come first, while yours dangles off the edge of their palm, to be tossed aside as soon as the smallest disturbance occurs.

With half a minute remaining before Sayari's launch, the voice of the person-machine sounded: "On the count of three... get ready to leave this world." And once this warning had been issued, he heard it counting: "ONE...TWO...THREE!" And then an immediate *fyuu*.

It looked like white tongues of flame were blasting from the belly of the Earth, enshrouding it and propelling Sayari into flight. It was a very intense blaze, visible even to those who'd closed their eyes. Meanwhile, inside, Dzombo was trying to catch his breath. His mind was racing with an unexpected euphoria. Soon he would close his eyes and sleep! But no, he instantly shook off that illusion. He remembered that this was Sayari taking off. When he least expected it, he would fall into an eternal sleep, right then and there. So he latched onto the wheel like a child at his mother's breast. Exerting all his power of mind and body, he was able to guide it toward that vertical arrow that would put Sayari on track. As soon as he managed this, the ship began soaring into the sky like a bird without wings.

Inside, it was a battle for survival. But outside, down on Earth, his relatives and the rest of the crowd were gazing up into the sky, anticipating his demise. The sign of death overhead: a plummeting wheel of flame. They were expecting an explosion, and then a scattering of ashes, just like always—but that's not what was happening now.

Indeed, it came as a great shock when they saw Sayari break away from this burning wheel and turn toward the unknown. If death was Dzombo's destination, then it seemed he had already left hell behind.

...Dzombo was one of those rare individuals who could shatter centuries of trickery, leaving the ignorant to assume his feat was some kind of miracle...

Straight up into the sky, he flew calmly. "God, I'm on my way," he spoke out loud to himself with an unbroken spirit. The moment he parted from the world's gravitational pull, he belonged to us no more. He knew he had left the world forever when he felt Sayari extricating itself, forcefully detaching from gravity, released like a child bursting forth from the womb in order to become a whole, free creature.

This womb bore him into outer space, into a universe with no edges. Down below, the world was reduced to a simple dot. That was when he quit ascending and started cruising. He stretched out facedown, making himself comfortable. He kept a firm hold on the wheel, pointing it in the direction of God's Heaven.

In front of him there was nothing. A world without an

end. "It's a long way to God," he told himself. In order to kill some time, he decided to poke around and learn more about the ship. First, he resumed reading about how to operate it. He focused on the three remaining instructions. There was no way of knowing when he would need them—but vigilance is readiness, not cowardice—as the saying goes in our world. And if this journey was truly Heaven-bound, then he'd better know how to handle whatever vehicles they had there.

Soon, he was gripped by hunger and thirst. His inspection had already revealed where the food and drink were stored. He tapped a few of the tubes, and their caps popped right off. They dangled in front of his face, waiting to be put in his mouth. Impressed, he sucked on the one labeled "ugali and kale."

"The other ones can wait; before I know it, I'll be eating manna," he said, to boost his spirit. The water was just regular water. In Heaven, there would be mineral water, and the Zamzam Well, too. Things he'd never tasted before in his entire life. Where he came from, that kind of water wasn't imbibed by regular folks, but by those who were known as *the big guys.* As far as the big guys were concerned, if they couldn't have mineral water, or something with flavor, then they wouldn't drink at all!

"Bigness is sickness, don't tell me!" he shouted at himself. But for now, he didn't drink anything, hoping to make himself as thirsty as possible by the time he got to Heaven. "There, I will find the water that quenches eternal thirst," he recited...

All this time, Sayari was just rumbling along, *shwaaa*...

Things were calm inside. The machine was running like it was supposed to. By now, Dzombo had forgotten all about dying, as he imagined getting a chance to explain himself before God... What would he say? Is God a woman or a man? Pure light or breath? Menacing or charming? Will God take my hand, or pass me over? He started to think about how he'd wound up here on this journey, his mind drifting all the way back to the world, as he confronted his own life story. He was rehearsing how he might tell it when, suddenly, he heard the blare of a warning siren.

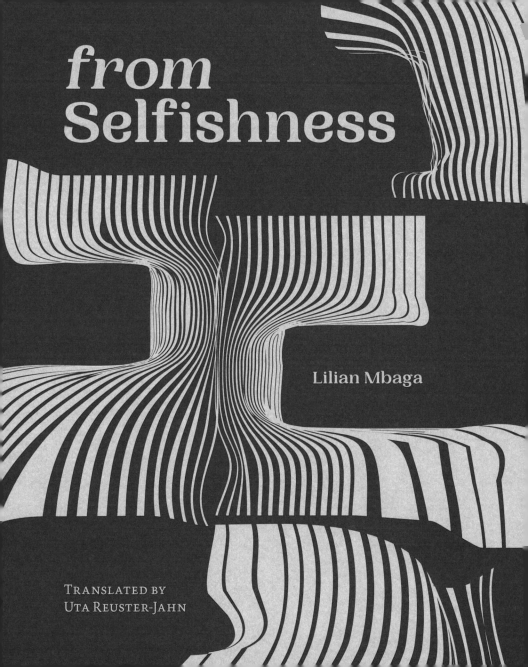

Mwanamkuu hakuelewa walihitaji
funguo kwa madhumuni yepi. Chumba
kilikuwa chake yeye na mume wake.
Ambaye, muda huo alikuwa katika
ulimwengu mwingine.

THE NEIGHBORHOOD CONSISTED OF ORDERLY ROWS OF houses. A street with a sidewalk ran through it. The gated houses had two separate entrances: a larger one for cars and a smaller one for those who arrived on foot. In front of each house, attractive and well-maintained flowers swayed in the wind, waving cheerfully to those passing by. This was right in the middle of Mbezi Beach, one of the more affluent neighborhoods in the city, where it was usually quiet. However, today there was a throng of cars and people.

What was going on?

On the left side of the street was a white house that was particularly eye-catching. Three tents had been set up in front, each one full of guests, some seated in chairs, others on woven palm mats. Others still were standing. Whispers could be heard here and there. After all, where people come together, there are conversations.

The men were primarily dressed in white *kanzu* robes
and wore embroidered *baraghashia* caps. About thirty women
were gathered in the fenced courtyard, many seated on
mats in a tent along the righthand side of the yard. Most of
them were wearing long *dera* dresses. In addition, they had
kanga cloths tied around their waists and over their heads
to cover themselves. The women too were talking quietly
among themselves.

Behind the house near the chicken coop stood several large
cooking pots, each propped on three stones, with logs burning
underneath. Food was being cooked here. The firewood was blazing vigorously, and a stately woman, tall and fat, was straining
to stir the pot's contents. For her, stirring thirty kilos was no
problem. The only thing that bothered her was the heat of Dar es
Salaam, which was intensified by the fire. In front of the chicken
coop, no less than six women were bent over, cutting onions.
Every few minutes, they had to stop to wipe away their tears
with the tips of their *kitenge* cloths. They cried without having
been beaten, though still not by choice.

The interior of the house was lavishly decorated, with
most walls painted a light pink. In the living room, the arm-
chairs had been pushed to the side, all without diminishing
the room's attractiveness. Wailing could be heard from one of
the bedrooms. The women in there were sitting on palm mats,

lamenting, several holding a hand to their cheek, their faces expressions of utter sorrow.

There was no question that they were crying. Their reddened eyes said it all; some had even become swollen.

Inside this bedroom, a woman sat leaning against the wall, her gaze fixed on the wall opposite, as if she were inspecting something. Tears streamed down her face and mucus ran from her nose to her chin. She didn't care. She didn't even bother to wipe her face. The cloth she had wrapped around her head now sat askew, but she didn't care about that either. Two girls were on either side of her, their heads in her lap. Both were crying softly.

They had all suffered a huge loss.

In the doorway to the bedroom stood a middle-aged man, his eyes wandering around the room. Next to him stood a woman, one hand resting on her hip, the other adjusting her black turban, which she'd worn especially for the funeral.

Miran had been lying on her mother's lap when she saw her *baba mkubwa*—her father's eldest brother—beckoning her over. Straightening up, she made her way to the door, and they began speaking in whispers. Then she returned to her mother.

"Mama, Ba'mkubwa said he wanted the key," Miran said in her childish voice.

"Key? What key?" asked her mother. She did not know,

or maybe didn't want to understand, which key he could possibly need. She ran her hand over her face, wiping away the tears she couldn't hold back.

"I don't know either, Mama," Miran replied, shrugging. When Mwanamkuu looked back toward the door, her brother-in-law was nowhere to be seen. She gave the matter no further thought and continued wailing.

"Mama Miran, we want the key," Semeni said now. Her voice had an edge to it, startling everyone in the room.

"Which key do you want? Miran told me, but I didn't understand," Mwanamkuu replied to her sister-in-law in a friendly tone. She stood up and went over to the doorway, where Semeni was standing. From the look on her face, it was clear it was no joke.

"The key to the deceased's bedroom."

"You mean the key to our bedroom, mine and my husband's?" she asked incredulously.

"That's the one," her sister-in-law replied, staring coldly back at her.

"Why do you need the key?" she asked, lowering her voice. She had a feeling that others were listening in on their conversation.

"What's so strange about it? It is our brother's room after all," her sister-in-law retorted full of disdain.

Mwanamkuu found it disturbing that they wanted the key. The bedroom was hers and her husband's. Her husband, who at this point was already in another world. An alarm bell was going off in her head. She tried hard not to give way to the bad feelings that were suddenly welling up inside her.

She looked at her sister-in-law, who was arrogantly tapping her foot on the floor to intimidate her, a clear sign that she was ready to fight. Mwanamkuu thought about just handing over the key, but her heart told her to wait. Why exactly did they need the key? Her sister-in-law had been evasive. Evidently, she did not want to tell her the truth or make her intentions known.

Mwanamkuu was at a loss of what to do, her head full of heavy thoughts.

At the sight of her brother-in-law returning, she felt some relief. "Brother-in-law, listen, the key—" she began, but her words were cut short by Mvanda's imperious voice.

"Hand over the key, woman!" he raged.

Her in-laws' faces showed no sign that they were joking. They were both glaring at her coldly.

"Could it be that everything I see in films is happening here right now? That when you become a widow, your in-laws suddenly seem turned inside out?" she asked herself. "No, no!" She banished such feelings from her thoughts. She saw no reason why her in-laws should behave this way. They hadn't looked at her with such coldness when their younger brother was still alive. Her husband. Surely this was all because of her husband's wealth. Or so she guessed. It stung her heart.

Making her way back into the room to rejoin the other mourners, she paused in the doorway.

"Miran, Miran," she called out, desperate. Once she'd gotten the girl's attention, she continued, "Listen, please go and call your grandfather."

Mwanamkuu leaned against the wall, sliding down until she was seated on the floor of the hallway. She could see her brother-in-law and sister-in-law whispering to each other. Straining her ears, she only managed to pick up a few morsels of their conversation. "She must give us the key," her brother-in-law muttered angrily. His eyes met hers briefly, but she quickly looked away.

"Ah, what's going on? Why are you over here? What's wrong?" Mzee Mshanga rained down a plethora of questions on his daughter.

"They want the key to our bedroom, mine and my husband's. I asked them why, but they won't say. I don't understand them," she replied, standing up.

Mzee Mshanga approached his daughter's in-laws. He spoke kindly to them, sharing words of wisdom. He tried to explain that it was not right to ask a widow for the key to her room so soon after her loss. But they did not seem to understand him. They persisted. They wanted the key, now.

Given Mzee Mshanga's age, their rude responses were completely inappropriate. As an old man, he understood well what this was all about. He took his daughter aside and instructed her to stay in the mourning room without handing over the key. Then they simply turned and left her in-laws standing there, fuming.

Not even a quarter of an hour had passed when a heavy thud rang out, frightening everyone. It was the sound of something breaking under brute force. It hurt their ears, and made them anxious. Mwanamkuu stood up quickly, her heart beating so fast she thought it might stop altogether.

Lahaula.

The door to her bedroom was being smashed in. Mwanamkuu just stood there, watching in utter disbelief.

They paid her no mind and just went on with their work. They were attempting to break down the door, having failed to get the key.

"Brother-in-law, what are you doing?" Mwanamkuu barely managed to get the words out. Her voice was trembling with fear. She got no answer. Instead, the heavy thuds of the hammer continued. It sure was being swung hard! It was obvious the door was no match for it and would give way at any moment.

Relatives from both sides were crowding into the corridor to see what was happening. Their presence did not prevent the door from being smashed. But it did cause an uproar. It was a wild mess!

Those on the husband's side of the family insisted that the door be broken down, while those on the wife's side tried valiantly to prevent it.

Tobaa! Suddenly, the door gave way!

Everyone rushed in. The husband's relatives were first through the door. Not one stayed behind. Those on the wife's side demanded to know what was going on. Those on the husband's side had no time to answer them, as they were already turning the room inside out.

All the wardrobe drawers were pulled out, as everything inside it was ransacked. But that was still not enough for them. They searched under the bed. The wife's relatives were helpless. What was happening before their eyes was worse than anything they'd seen in films. The others continued with the operation. Clothes were thrown here and there, the husband's clothes packed into a large *shangazi-kaja* bag.

"Take any papers that seem important to you," said Mvanda, who was covered in sweat from breaking down the door, as he walked back over to the wardrobe. He and his companions had no time to check what was important or unimportant. They simply took everything with them to sort through later.

The wife's relatives could only intervene with words. "Leave this, leave that." Or: "You'll break the table!" Still others: "Don't break that mirror!" Poor them, their cries didn't help them in the least! It only made the pillagers angrier, as they searched through everything they could.

At this point the wife of the deceased left the room, sobbing. First her husband had died and now look what was happening. What could she do? Her father was too old. He wouldn't be able to hold back all those stronger, younger men. Instead, it was Mwanamkuu's eldest son, Mtao, who took up the fight.

"Let go, I told you...these are my father's," Mtao protested, but his baba mkubwa pushed him aside without bothering to respond. Mtao lost his balance and, after failing to catch himself, banged his head on the edge of the table. At the sound of her son's scream, Mwanamkuu jumped to her feet, as the room devolved into total chaos. Her wails intensified when she saw her son lying on the floor bleeding. It was not apparent whether he was alive or dead.

Her late husband's relatives took no notice. They continued carting away what they considered to be theirs.

"Get out of here! We don't want to see you ever again. If you're wise, you'll leave here today!" her sister-in-law said haughtily, looking right at Mwanamkuu, who was crying, shaken by the sight of her son bleeding from the head and shoulder.

"Here, take these. I want to get these insurgents out of here first," Mvanda said, handing a stack of papers to Semeni.

So her brother-in-law was chasing them out of the house. Mwanamkuu looked at Mvanda. She wished she had the courage to defend herself, but she felt utterly powerless. Apart from the death of her husband, there was now the condition of her son Mtao to worry about. It made her heart heavy with grief.

All her children were crying now. Mtao was their big brother at twenty-two years old. Sixteen-year-old Miran was trying hard to calm her sister Laura who, at fourteen, was the third eldest. And crouching by his mother was nine-year-old Akil, the youngest. Akil touched his big brother's face, calling his name.

Then the boy looked at Mvanda, their baba mkubwa, but Mvanda paid them no attention, continuing with his mission to drive them out of the house.

"You, be quiet! He's not dead, and even if he were, who would care!" Mvanda left the room, returning with a bowl of water. *Pwaa!* He dumped the water on the face of the unconscious Mtao, who began to move and opened his eyes, squinting. Soon he had regained full consciousness.

The whole mess gave rise to much talk. It had been free,

albeit distressing, cinema for those present. Mzee Mshanga had been unable to put an end to the chaos. And strangely, none of the other mourners had dared to intervene either.

But shortly afterward, the elders conferred on the sidelines, calling Mzee Mshanga to join them. The funeral was being derailed. The elders agreed that it was their duty to do what they could to reduce the tension.

And so, after their brief consultation, they intervened and managed to deescalate the situation somewhat. They asked Mvanda and his cronies to accommodate the family of their deceased brother, at least until the funeral was over. Eventually, they agreed to postpone all further talks and negotiations until the deceased had been buried in his eternal resting place.

Although this eased the tension somehow, it was not enough to heal the aching hearts of Mwanamkuu, her children, and her relatives.

To be ousted on the day before her husband's burial!

Mwanamkuu still could not believe it. Was she dreaming? She tried hard to process what had happened and what it meant for her future, but her heart went numb, leaving her completely depressed and in pain. The world seemed a bitter place to her.

"Dear God! Why would you let this happen to me?" Mwanamkuu cried, but only her children could hear her.

TRANSLATED BY
DUNCAN IAN TARRANT

Euphrase Kezilahabi

from
Nagona

Mara, mahali fulani karibu nao,
waliona kitu fulani kikijiviringisha
ndani ya vumbi halafu ghafla mtu
aliibuka akiwa ameenea vumbi jeupe.
Yule mtu alianza kupiga kelele.

DRYNESS EVERYWHERE. WHITE DUST LIKE LIME HAD settled on the ground. The drum players were sitting in a circle singing "*Utenzi wa Kiyama*—The Utenzi of Judgement Day." Now and then, the dust would be blown into their eyes. But they simply rubbed their eyes and continued to sing. Suddenly, somewhere nearby, something stirred and spun in the dust; then, just as suddenly, someone burst into existence in an explosion of white dust. The new arrival began to shout.

"Get away from *Cogito*! There is no *causa ultima* in the circle! What we need is *disciplina voluntatis*!" The person stopped shouting upon seeing the drummers. "Who are you?"

"We are drummers," answered one of the drummers.

"Why are you here in a place where you are not expected?"

"Where is *here*?" they asked.

"If I knew, I wouldn't be here to reveal the secret of my craft! This song of yours, what is it called?"

"We will know when the Master stands in the center of the circle," responded another. "We're just now learning our first song."

"And where are your dancers?"

"They are any who can think," answered another. "But the good dancers are those who overcome that limitation and enter the free world. We don't get many of them. Many come claiming that they know. They suit us just fine, they're good for a laugh."

"So, you are where you are expected to be," the arrival from the dust said. "I, too, am a dancer. I was in the middle of practicing the hallucinations that I'll perform on the Day of the Great Dance."

At these words, another person burst suddenly out of the dust, appearing a short ways from where they were. He screamed and caused the dust to swirl around.

"A great discovery! A great discovery has been made of the soul!" He stopped suddenly when he saw the others.

"And what are you all doing here?! The words I just uttered should not be heard by any creature who is not conscious. But seeing as you, who have souls, have heard my words, what do you make of them?"

"Nonsense!" said the first to have appeared out of the dust. "You can't separate the soul from the body!"

"I, too, used to think like that," responded the second arrival.

"But ever since I lost my soul, I've stopped worrying about it."

"How did you lose it?" asked the first.

"I was ordered to clean it at a specific spot in the River of Eternal Life. It got away from me and the current carried it off to the great ocean where dreams end."

"What was it like before it escaped you?"

"A stupor of being fixated on something worthless."

"How long had you held onto it?"

"Every day up until I was forgotten."

"How do you feel now?"

"Free! Completely free! If you want, I can also show you the path to take in order to lose your soul!" At this, the first arrival began to tremble. He ran away shouting, "I don't want to be forgotten before the Great Dance!" The second arrival followed close at his heels: "I'll show you how to lose your soul! Don't be materialistic! Be free!"

The drummers watched the two figures until they disappeared out of sight. Then they began learning their second song, "*Utenzi Baada ya Kiyama*—The Utenzi After Judgement Day."

*

It was the dead of night when Mother came to my *kibanda* to fetch me. I was still in amazement at the dream I had just had. I wasn't sure whether it was just a dream or whether it had actually happened. I remember being told to clean my soul. "Quickly!" Mother said again from outside. I got up hurriedly and put on my trousers and a shirt. I jumped at the sound of an owl hooting above the hut where I had been sleeping. As soon as I stepped outside, the owl flew off. All around me was darkness. I jumped again, this time at Mother's voice nearby: "Follow me." After a few steps, her voice trembling, Mother asked me, "How strong is your heart?" Never in my whole life had she asked me such a question. I didn't know the answer. The question was already complex enough when she added, "Hold onto your soul. That is truly what it is to grow up." In complete silence, we walked to my babu's hut. There was a light on inside.

In the house, we found Babu lying on his back, staring at the ceiling. Father sat at his feet, on the edge of the bed. He watched the patient's face closely. There were four of us altogether; me, Mother, Father, and the patient. Babu turned his head to look at me. Then, in a weak voice: "Your star, I see it, but from afar. Its light has dimmed, but it's strong enough to lead you to the place I told you about." He paused, letting out a long breath. Father was shocked. Now I understood Mother's words. I'd never seen someone die before. I had never seen how the soul leaves. Suddenly, Babu lifted his head as if he had seen something. His eyes shifted to the wall. His whole body began to shake. He was sweating. He closed his eyes. Slowly, he lay his head back down on the pillow. Like someone in a trance, he began to talk again.

"They will talk. I know they will talk. Some will say I taught nonsense. Others will call me a liar. But the way is completely open. It has nothing to do with being a genius or an idiot. They were all angry when I called them dancers." Silence followed. We listened to his breathing, confirmation that he was still alive. When the first rooster crowed, we were all very drowsy. When the first birds of dawn began their chorus, he spoke, asking a question.

"What did the priest do to me?

"When you refused to be baptised, he left."

"Good. He's one of the fools. It's good that he left before pouring that water on me. It would have made my thoughts meaningless for you all." He tried to sit up in bed, but his body did not have the strength. His efforts started to give us hope that he was getting better.

That's when the neighbors started coming to check on us. They greeted the patient and he responded for his part. This gave them hope too, so they left for their fields to continue with their daily work. That morning, Mother also went over to our farm to harvest some potatoes for lunch. Father had some time to go buy fish for the patient. Before he left, Father told me:

"Listen to your babu. Check on him regularly. If he gets worse, run quickly to get your mother in the field. But it seems he's not doing too badly at the moment."

Once both had left, I went back into the patient's room. My mouth and ears were open, waiting for the last breath to fall. When I entered, he lifted his head from the pillow. Then, as if he was looking at me, he smiled and lay back down slowly. He continued looking at the ceiling as he spoke.

"Where is your mother?"

"In the field."

"And your father?"

"He went to the market."

"Good. Is it light outside?"

"The sun is shining a bit, but it's misty."

"Mist? Can people see?"

"Yes, but not as far as on a normal day."

"The Guardians of Light are drawing near."

"The Guardians of Light?"

"You want to know much. They will arrive. If not today, then tomorrow." He turned his face to look at me. "I'm dying," he said. I was shocked to hear him say that. He bared his teeth in a grimace of extreme pain.

"Does it hurt?" I asked him. He smiled.

"There is no pain in dying. There is sadness and grief.

Sadness for all the wealth and the people you're leaving behind and for everything you never got the chance to do. But me, what wealth am I leaving behind? None. Perhaps my words. Who am I leaving behind? No one except you, your father, and your mother. You all understand me and are enlightened. You will not betray me. Everything I wanted to achieve, I achieved. I had enough time." Silence followed.

"Give me water," he said after running his tongue over his dry lips. I had been given instructions not to give him too much water. I gave him a little. He watched me mournfully as he took the cup. He drank some slowly, with great effort. When he gave me back the cup, he looked me in the eyes. "You're worried and afraid," he said.

"Aren't you worried?" I asked him.

"Fear is only felt by someone who desires to live a life they haven't yet lived."

"A life they haven't yet lived?"

"Life after death. I don't have that desire. Life is a wondrous thing. There are no steps before or after life, just during. If you don't know where you came from and you don't remember, what use is wanting to know where you're going?"

"They say we come from God and we return to God."

"Who?"

"Religious people."

"That's one of the songs that is sung in the dance of life. It's a beautiful song though." Silence again. This time for slightly longer.

"Give me your hand," he said, after a while. "Sit on the bed and look at me. This could be our last chance to be together and talk. Tell me one thing. Who do you want to be in your life?" This was a question I had asked myself many times.

"You don't have any plans for your future?!" he followed up, after I failed to respond quickly. "You don't?!"

"I would like to be a teacher."

"Ahaa," he said. A short silence followed, then he carried on, "Never teach anything about which you are not certain, and don't claim to hold the truth in your hands." Slowly, he let go of my hand. He said something, but I couldn't hear what. Babu looked at me. He could tell I needed to know what he had said. He repeated the word. This time slightly louder.

"Nagona? What does that mean?" I asked.

"Your ears are sharp. Anyone who is able to think has gotten to know her."

"I'm not sure if I have gotten to know her."

"You are already in the circle. You need only wait for the sign."

At that point, I heard Mother dropping off the potatoes outside. I heard her footsteps approaching.

"How is your babu doing?"

"Not so bad."

"Hasn't your father returned from the market yet?"

"He'll be back, Mother,"

"Let your babu rest a little now. You shouldn't make him talk so much when he's hungry." I hesitated to leave. "You have always been close to him. You still haven't had enough of his words."

"Let him stay with me," said Babu. "Without him I wouldn't be doing so well." As Mother was going out, Babu yawned long and wide, then said: "'*Maisha hayatakwisha bali watu waishao.*' Have you read that poem about living and dying?"

"Not yet."

"Read it." But before I could ask the name of the poet, he continued, "It's a very good poem. Do you read poetry?"

"Yes. A little."

He yawned again and said, "'*Wakati titi la nyati, hukamuliwa kwa shaka.*' Have you read that poem about milking a nursing buffalo?"

"Not yet."

"Read it as well. I am close to spitting out the buffalo's teat."

Again, like someone in a trance, he started talking, "You are the witness. I told them! The problem is that people no longer think. What is needed is someone who can revive this characteristic. But what did they say? Seize him! He's teaching nonsense! The old man's stick has made him weaker. Maybe, if you become a teacher, you can make your students think. Someone has to start." Father's voice could be heard outside. He greeted Mother, then I heard them rushing to prepare food. I looked at Babu. He was drowsy.

He didn't eat much lunch. He tasted a little bit of fish before asking for some gruel. After drinking the gruel, he fell back to sleep. This was not a happy day. The word *death* had found a place to hide in the backs of our minds. It reared up every time I tried to forget it. He slept little that evening. The neighbors who came by to check his status left with high hopes for his recovery.

It was not so. He rallied a few minutes before we usually went to bed. When we came into his room, he looked at me and said, "We still have time. I want to say something." He paused, silent, then spoke with great tiredness.

"Ahaa! Nagona! All my life she has caused me trouble. I saw her often from afar. I got close to her only a few times, but I never had the opportunity to catch her in my arms. Always, she escaped backward, leaving me to continue after her, drawn by some force. When I was lazy in my thinking, she lost me completely, but then she appeared again when I began thinking carefully. I watched thieves who managed to catch her, but she always escaped them. This advice is all a hallu-cination. We no longer see that which has been laid bare. We have become madmen in our efforts to reveal that which has already been revealed. My grandson, your star is beautiful. Perhaps you will be blessed and get to see her and seize her in your arms."

"But Babu, who is this Nagona?"

"You will see her, and when you see her, you will be surprised that you never saw her alongside you all this time. The important things are thought, will, and purpose. Why am I explaining all this to you, when I failed to catch her myself even at the end? I don't want to make you lose hope. I want you to be someone who loves trying."

"When and where did you see her?"

"She is everywhere. I saw her when I was half asleep and half awake, when I was fixated on thought and saw more than thought, half conscious, when I was relaxed, at a time of great suffering."

"This Nagona, what does she look like?"

"Nagona is light. Like the sun eclipsed by the moon. If you look too long, you'll go blind and see nothing else the rest of your life. But miraculously, you will be drawn to look without protecting yourself against her dangers. Once you see her, the desire to keep looking at her never ends. If she disappears, you'll keep hunting for her everywhere without fear."

"If I see her, how will I recognize her?"

"In the light you can't help but look at. When she's there, falsehood is removed, and she is the only thing left. You will find yourself drawn to her. But she will not allow you to seize her for yourself, because she belongs to everyone. Everyone recognizes her; because she pulls and prepares, we are pulled and prepared. No one can escape her pull."

"When should I expect to see and touch her?"

"I've told you many times already! There will be a sign."

"When and where will this sign appear?"

Babu looked at me. Then he turned his head to the ceiling and said, "The day of the accident in the valley of experts. A riddle was created there by the Guardians of Light when they slept." Silence followed. At that point, we heard people shouting from outside, over by all the termite mounds.

"*Zogwe! Zogwe! Zogwe!*" which means "Come and see!" Mother and I went outside. Lanterns hung above almost all the termite mounds. The shouting increased and could be heard throughout the village. The children who had been woken up started shouting, "Bring buckets! There's too many!" After a short while, every lantern next to every mound had been lit to welcome the termite guests who came out only once a year.

"Let's go back inside," said Mother. "Today is a dark day."

When we came in, Babu asked us, "I hear shouting, what's going on?

"The termites," answered Mother.

"Ah!" said Babu, "Today the Guardians of Light have banded together."

"Who are these Guardians?" I asked.

"Ants," he answered. A short silence followed, then he asked, "How many lanterns are there?"

"A lot. There's one next to each termite mound."

"Ah!" he said again. "And so it should always be." There was silence in the room. Outside the shouting continued.

At midnight, the patient's condition deteriorated quickly. His eyes started flicking from side to side. He wanted to say something, but his lips were too heavy. He tried again. In a weak voice, he spoke out: "My grandchild. Make sure you don't get trampled on the Day of the Great Dance. Always follow the circle and keep your eyes fixed on the center. When the center erupts, many things that have been hidden for centuries will be revealed." Something began rasping in his throat. With difficulty he said, "Nag... Nag... Nag..." He couldn't say another word. His eyes closed. His whole body fell still. I felt like someone was playing a joke on me. But those really were his last words. We covered him well. The wailing began. When the neighbors heard, they knew. They came to grieve with us.

Mother's wails mingled with the shouts of the people outside still collecting termites. We bowed our heads in unison like guards saluting a passing king. One of the termites found a way in through the window. It circled the lantern. Another termite entered, then a third, and they too flew in a circle. One of them flew down through a hole in the mosquito net and landed near the lantern's flame. I watched as first its wings burned off and it died; then it dried out like charcoal, its aroma perfuming the room.

My eyelids grew heavy. After a while my head started to nod with an uncertain tiredness. When I jolted back awake, Mother's wailing was still drawing tears from even the driest of eyes. I'd never experienced such a long night. We grieved through our grogginess. The termites, too, increased in number, flying in a circle around the light above, pulling us into their orbit whenever we watched them. The termites were like new planets being discovered for the first time. As we circled around the light, we were like dancers learning the steps to a difficult funeral song. But Mother continued to recite praises of the deceased. When the early morning birds began singing songs that called the witches back to their houses, Father told me sadly, "Turn off the lantern. We should save some oil for tomorrow." Then he turned to Mother. "Go rest. Save the moisture of your tears. New termite mounds are still being built."

When I went next door to get water from the kitchen to rinse my eyes, I noticed termites all over the ground, crawling along in pairs without their wings. Many were already digging themselves into the soil. I remembered that some believe termites grow to be trees. In the distance, I could see children pulling up every new shoot that had broken out of the ground.

Where the sun rose and its rays began to burn, there were also signs of rain. But a rainbow appeared and the likelihood of it raining waned. When our relatives arrived and the grave was ready, we buried him in the village graveyard on the hill. After the burial, as the funeral party started home, it began to drizzle although the sun was still shining. People said, "Today, the leopard has given birth."

This all took place a long time ago when I was still a child. I was fourteen years old when Babu passed away. It was the night of termites and the Guardians of Light. I remember now after many years of forgetfulness and hallucinations. Ah!

Contributors

Lusajo Mwaikenda Israel is a Tanzanian writer who received his degree in fine and performing arts from the University of Dar es Salaam. He further pursued his Master's in Community Development (MCED) at Open University of Tanzania and a postgraduate diploma in education at Teofilo Kisanji University. In the 1990s, he was a founding member of Daz Nundaz, a pioneering group of the Bongo Flava and Swahili hip-hop musical genres.

Hassan Kassim is a Kenyan writer and Kiswahili literary translator living in Mombasa. In 2020, he was longlisted for the Toyin Falola prize for African short fiction. His work is published or forthcoming in *Lolwe*, *Sahifa Journal*, Writers Space Africa's *Twaweza* anthology, Lunaris's *In The Sands of Time* anthology, among others.

Euphrase Kezilahabi (1944–2020) was a Tanzanian novelist, poet, playwright, and philosopher. Kezilahabi wrote in an everyday Swahili for the masses while simultaneously conveying complex ideas about societal alienation and liberation. Despite not always being accepted by his contemporaries, especially regarding his controversial free verse poetry, today, as Annmarie Drury states in the foreword to her translation of his poetry, he's accepted as "a key figure of modernization and democratization, a renovator of the Swahili literary tradition."

Idza Luhumyo is a writer from Kenya and winner of the 2022 Caine Prize for African Writing.

Mwas Mahugu is a Sheng writer and an Afro-hip hop artist who, when not singing, writes, coordinates music events, and manages artists. His Sheng writing was first published by *Kwani?* in 2005. Later *Kwani?* featured his work in three more publications. Mwas is also a founding member of Jalada Africa, a pan-African writers collective based in Kenya. As a pioneer Sheng writer, he cofounded *Tribe 43*—a one-page Sheng magazine featured on *People Daily* and now in its fifth year. Mwas writes to discover and loves to capture real life street experiences in his writing.

Enock Matundura teaches Kiswahili literature at Chuka University, Kenya. He is a translator and creative writer, mostly of Kiswahili children's literature and short stories. His book *Sitaki Iwe Siri* [It shouldn't be a secret, Longhorn, 2008] was a runner-up for the 2009 Text Book Centre Jomo Kenyatta Literature Pize. He translated the Moses Series by renowned young adult literature writer Barbrara Kimenye into Kiswahili, all published by Oxford University Press. Matundura also runs a weekly column in *Taifa Leo*, the only Kiswahili newspaper in Kenya, and has contributed articles to the *Saturday Nation* and *Sunday Nation*.

Lilian Mbaga, born 1991, addresses gender inequality in Tanzania in her writing. Her first book, *Tabasamu la Uchungu* (Smile of bitterness, 2014), recounts a girl's trauma from rape. Her second novel *Hatinafsi* (Selfishness, 2018) deals with a widow's harassment and dispossession by her in-laws. Given the difficult Tanzanian publishing environment, Mbaga has self-published her books. *Hatinafsi* came to prominence by promotion through the new writers' association UWARIDI of which Mbaga is a member. In 2021, she also participated in a very successful collaborative online novel about sextortion by five writers of the association.

Katama G. C. Mkangi (1944–2004) was a novelist, activist, and sociologist born in southeast Kenya, best known for his three novels, *Ukiwa* (1975), *Mafuta* (1984), and *Walenisi* (1995). He came by his interest in political satire honestly; under the regime of

President Daniel arap Moi, Mkangi was held as a political prisoner from 1986 to 1988 for his association with the underground Mwakenya Movement that agitated for multiparty democracy.

Clara Momanyi is a Kenyan academic, creative writer, and translator who has been teaching Kiswahili literature in Kenyan universities for many years. Her creative works include novels such as *Tumaini* (Hope), *Nakuruto*, and *Nguu za Jadi* (Old summits). Some of her children's books include *Ushindi wa Nakate* (Nakate's Victory), which won the 2015 Text Book Centre Jomo Kenyatta Prize for Literature; *Siku ya Wajinga* (Fools' day); and *Pendo Katika Shari* (Love in adversity). She has also written several Kiswahili short stories, which have appeared in various Kiswahili short story anthologies. Professor Momanyi has also published numerous academic papers in peer-reviewed journals in Africa, Asia, and Europe.

Fadhy Mtanga, from Tanzania, has published five novels, a poetry collection, and various uncollected short stories. His narratives, featuring people from various walks of life and socioeconomic classes, reflect on and weave together relationship issues, family issues, and matters related to work, power, and authority. Through his use of staccato sentences, introduction of new vocabulary, and subtle incorporation of

English words and phrases, Fadhy Mtanga's writing has contributed significantly to the development of modern Swahili.

Richard Prins is a New Yorker who has lived, worked, studied, and recorded music in Dar es Salaam. He received his MFA degree in poetry from New York University, and he is currently completing an MFA in literary translation at Queens College. His poems, essays, and translations of Swahili poetry have appeared in publications such as *Gulf Coast*, *jubilat*, and *Ploughshares*, and received "Notable" mentions in *Best American Essays* and *Best American Travel Writing*.

Uta Reuster-Jahn is a lecturer in Swahili language and literature at the University of Hamburg, Germany. She obtained her certificate of Higher Swahili in Tanzania in 1987 while living in the country. She has translated the novel *Titi la Mkwe* (1972) by Tanzanian author Alex Banzi (1945–2021) into German (*Versuchung*, 2016). In addition, she has widely published on the topics of translation of Swahili literature and Swahili popular culture.

Jay Boss Rubin studied Swahili at the University of Dar es Salaam and has an MFA in literary translation from Queens College. In 2021, he was awarded a PEN/Heim Translation Fund

Grant to enable the completion of his translation of the classic Swahili novel *Rosa Mistika* by Euphrase Kezilahabi. He's held a wide variety of teaching, translating, and interpreting positions, and he also writes fictions of his own, in English.

Fatma Shafii is a Kiswahili writer from the Kenyan Coast. Her short fiction and poems have appeared in *Lolwe*, *Jalada Africa*, and SHIWAKI: an organization she founded that aims to increase institutional support for Kiswahili writing and writers. Other published works include a short story in the anthology *Waterbirds on the Lakeshore*, a Goethe-Institut anthology of Afro young adult fiction which has been published in French, English, and Kiswahili.

Duncan Ian Tarrant spent the first five years of his life in the DR Congo, before his family moved back to the UK. As such, he has always loved cultural exchange, which led him to study at SOAS, London, and the University of Bayreuth, Germany, where he is now doing his PhD in Swahili Literature. Aside from his passion for literature, Duncan also plays ultimate frisbee, enjoys live music, and loves hiking with his girlfriend.

CALICO

The Calico Series, published biannually by
Two Lines Press, captures vanguard works
of translated literature in stylish, collectible
editions. Each Calico is a vibrant snapshot
that explores one aspect of our present
moment, offering the voices of previously
inaccessible, highly innovative writers from
around the world today.